Jack Vance

The Flesh Mask

Jack Vance

The Flesh Mask

John Holbrook Vance

Spatterlight Press Signature Series, Volume 14

Published by Spatterlight Press

Cover art by Howard Kistler

ISBN 978-1-61947-146-7

Spatterlight Press LLC

340 S. Lemon Ave #1916
Walnut, CA 91789

www.jackvance.com

Take My Preface

Jack Vance's *The Flesh Mask* (1957) has origins in his earlier lost novel *Cold Fish,* written in 1948. The 1940s were a gestational period for Vance's craft, and just as his famous fantasy *Mazirian the Magician* begins the "bright path" of Vance's work, so does *The Flesh Mask* debut his dark path.

The Flesh Mask is set in "San Giorgio," a fictional town lying sixty miles north of San Francisco. The locale does not seem to be coastal, nor does it seem part of the wine country in nearby Napa Valley, so the area around Santa Rosa seems like a good fit. San Giorgio is a bucolic landscape serving as both a playground for the country-club squires and a hardscrabble for the least fortunate.

As more than fifty years have passed since the original publication date of 1957, a little historical context is in order. Although the novel makes no mention of the Great Depression (1929-39), its main character Robert Struve, born in 1930, is obviously a child of it: the first nine years of his life find his nation in a grinding economic mess, and then comes World War Two. (While the novel says nothing about the war, Robert has a life-changing day on July 17, 1944, coincidentally the date of the Port Chicago Disaster, a massive munitions explosion in the Sacramento River Delta about twenty miles from Vance's childhood home of Oakley.) Due to his early life experience, Robert has a skeptical view toward the post-war boom years that he finds around him as a young adult.

The Flesh Mask is an early Vance work containing many elements used throughout his career, but one thing it lacks is humor, a trait that contributes to its "dark path" nature. A staple in most of his work,

Vancean humor has several modes, from slapstick, to sly social satire, to ribald traveler's tales. Vancean humor can be as dry as James Branch Cabell's wit, as cutting as Ambrose Bierce's sarcasm, or as lighthearted as P.G. Wodehouse's levity. There is none of this in *The Flesh Mask,* making it hardboiled Vance.

Other milestones along Vance's dark path include *Bad Ronald* (1973) and *The Four Johns* (1964; the preferred title being "Strange She Hasn't Written"), one of his Ellery Queen novels. With the aforementioned lack of Vancean humor, the main component to Vance's dark path is a gruesome horror. This might seem axiomatic, if one believes that humor and horror do not mix, yet with Vance's fiction humor and horror often go together quite well. This can be illustrated with a simple sample from *Mazirian the Magician* showing how Vance's bright path method can still treat gruesome horror with humor, however paradoxical that might seem: witness the case of Liane the Wayfarer. When combat woman T'sais first sees this character (in "T'sais" of *Mazirian the Magician*) she thinks him "slightly less ignoble" than his two prisoners, even somewhat "elegant." Then Liane proceeds to torture the couple in a cheerful manner, until the heroine T'sais is moved to intervene.

(Granted that this example uses humor to show Liane's "artistic" sadism, but Vance is not limited to this particular form in mixing humor and horror.)

So, Dear Reader, in *The Flesh Mask* you will encounter:

- A picture-perfect town with class tensions roiling beneath the manicured surface.
- An individual tormented first by blind bad luck, then by cruel human cupidity.
- A mystery plot balancing between simple complexity and complex simplicity.

In short, get ready for a new type of Vance novel: humorless, hardboiled, and gritty. It is the first step of his dark path, a side less seen.

—*Michael Andre-Driussi*

Chapter I

Robert Struve, age thirteen, differed only in detail from his friends. He read comic books; wore jeans and sports shirts.

His father, Bradley, was dead; he lived with his mother, Elsbeth, in the top half of a stucco duplex. Elsbeth Cranleigh was of good Philadelphia stock, willowy, blonde, rather pale. In 1928 Bradley, representing himself as a soldier of fortune, had swept her off her feet. He talked big money and madcap adventure; Elsbeth had taken him at his word, but after their marriage there was none of the romance and gaiety she had expected. For several years Bradley sold real estate in Los Angeles, then, in 1934, he brought Elsbeth and four-year-old Robert to San Giorgio, sixty miles north of San Francisco. He sold vacuum cleaners for two years, worked briefly for a polling organization, then went back into real estate. He had an easy tongue, a debonair laugh, a Los Angeles-style mustache; he knew a hundred smutty stories; still, he failed to make much headway.

Elsbeth's illusions vanished, but she clung to her hopes.

When Robert was eight Bradley went to work for Hovard Orchards as night manager of the San Giorgio warehouse. He held the job three months, until Darrell Hovard found him drunk on the job for the second time in two weeks. Hovard paid him off on the spot. Bradley drove down the highway in a reckless fury, and at Dead Man's Bend sideswiped a lumber truck.

Elsbeth quickly adjusted to widowhood. She had married not Bradley but the idea of Bradley — strong, gay, gallant, resourceful. The discord vanished with Bradley's death.

"Darling," she told Robert the morning after the terrible event, "you've got to be very brave. God has taken your father from us."

"Is he really dead, Mother? I bet he was drunk."

"Why do you say an awful thing like that, Robert?"

Robert was silent.

"Why, Robert?"

"It was the kids," Robert blurted out. "They told me Daddy was gonna drink himself to death."

"What a terrible thing to say!" Elsbeth gasped. "Your daddy was one of the finest men that ever walked this earth!"

Robert said nothing. Elsbeth continued in her soft voice: "You must always remember that, Robert dear. And now that Daddy's gone — you'll have to be the man in the house. You'll have to be brave and strong and help Mummy."

Robert's throat was swollen and his eyes were stinging. "I will, Mummy. I'll do anything you want."

So Robert became man of the family. He found the position no sinecure. Elsbeth went to work at Hegenbel's, San Giorgio's largest department store, at a barely sufficient salary. Robert learned that he must earn a lot of money as soon as possible. He learned, "Grit, Robert, stick-to-itiveness, that's the way to get ahead!"

Robert was a handsome boy, with black hair, innocent hazel eyes, a fresh young skin. He enjoyed no particular prestige among his contemporaries; he was neither ugly like Grant Hovard, fat like Ducky Scheib, truculent like Jim Smith. He lacked Ziggy Gordon's loud voice and high spirits, Carr Pendry's impetuous recklessness.

He bought a bicycle with earnings from his paper route, and thereafter gave everything to Elsbeth, who started what she called his 'college fund'.

Carr Pendry also delivered a paper route. His father published the San Giorgio *Herald-Republican*, and had some notion of starting Carr at the bottom.

Carr, a year older than Robert, owned a new motor-scooter which, from time to time, he allowed Robert to ride. On such days Robert delivered Carr's papers as well as his own.

Carr's route included exclusive Jamaica Terrace, where the Hovards, the Pendrys, the McDermotts, the Cloverbolts and the Hegenbels lived in large old-fashioned houses. Whenever Robert delivered Carr's route he told himself that he and his mother would someday own a house on Jamaica Terrace.

And then Darrell Hovard's Cadillac, with little Julie Hovard sitting between her father's legs steering, rumbled like a monstrous beetle through Jamaica Arch, and ran into Robert on the motor-scooter.

The motor-scooter tumbled into a culvert. Robert's head struck the concrete; gasoline gushed over him, into his face, and caught on fire.

Darrell Hovard held Julie's head down when the body of Robert Struve, charred and moaning, was lifted into the ambulance.

"Hush now," muttered Hovard. "Be quiet. We're going home..." And he said to himself, "Thank God for insurance..."

The adjuster found Elsbeth Struve at the hospital; he was Edward D. Cooley, a thin young man with a crew cut. He approached Elsbeth in the hall outside Robert's hospital room. The doctor had promised a report on Robert's condition in a few minutes, and she hardly noticed when Edward Cooley took a seat beside her.

"A terrible business," said Cooley.

Elsbeth looked at him, seeing little more than a blur. "Yes, yes."

"Naturally, you'll have nothing to worry about in regard to the doctor bills. We'll take care of this emergency treatment."

Elsbeth took a sidelong look at the sharp-faced young man. He seemed grave and concerned. "Who are you?"

"I represent the insurance company. I've come to help you straighten things out."

"Oh," said Elsbeth. "I still don't know anything about it. Except that Robert had an accident on a motor-scooter and Mr. Hovard brought him in."

Cooley nodded. "That's right. Mr. Hovard's insurance covers the contingency, and we've agreed to take care of Robert's hospital care. But we'll need your permission to pay the bill, a release."

"Oh, certainly." Elsbeth laughed weakly.

"Then — let's see — I have a release somewhere." Edward Cooley felt in his breast pocket. "You'd better sign this... right here."

Elsbeth took his pen.

The doctor came out of Robert's room with a nurse; the two held a whispered conversation. Elsbeth thrust pen and paper back to Cooley, jumped to her feet. But before Elsbeth could reach him, the doctor hurried away.

The nurse said, "Mrs. Struve?"

"Yes... Robert — can I see him?"

The nurse shook her head. "He's under sedatives. He wouldn't recognize you, and frankly, Mrs. Struve, I don't think it would be wise right now."

"Is he — Is he —"

"No — he'll pull through — but he's had some very bad burns... Perhaps you'd better wait a day or so."

Elsbeth looked at the white door, so firmly closed. "He won't be marked, will he?" she asked hesitantly.

"We'll do our best, Mrs. Struve —"

Elsbeth turned away. Edward Cooley stepped up. "All I need is your signature on this settlement, then we can take care of all the bills."

"Please," said Elsbeth, "not right now."

Cooley followed her. "But, Mrs. Struve..."

"I don't want to sign anything until I can read it..."

Edward Cooley drove out Conroy Avenue toward Jamaica Terrace. At the arch he found Carr Pendry inspecting the wreck of his motorscooter. Cooley stopped the car, jumped out on the sidewalk. "Quite an accident."

"Yeah," said Carr. "That's what's left of my scooter. Almost new."

"I suppose you're insured?" Cooley inquired jocularly.

Carr shook his head, glanced sourly up Jamaica Terrace. "But old Hovard's got insurance. If it's any good."

"All insurance is good," said Cooley.

Carr looked at him skeptically. "Even when his little girl is driving?"

Cooley ducked his head like a heron after a minnow. "What's that?"

"I said, 'even when his little girl's driving'."

"Well, well," said Cooley. "The little girl was driving?"

Carr nodded. "Old Hovard lets her drive all the time. Lets her do anything."

"Well, well..." Cooley climbed back into his car.

He pressed the bell button at the Hovard home, and a colored maid opened the door. "Yes, sir?"

"Mr. Darrell Hovard, please."

"You got an appointment? Mr. Hovard's not feeling so good."

"I'm Edward Cooley of the Magna Insurance Company. Mr. Hovard reported an accident."

"I'll see if he's home."

Mr. Hovard was home. The maid led Cooley down a cool red-tiled hall, past glass doors leading into living room, dining room, library; past fine spiral stairs sweeping up to the second floor. On the third step Julie sat hugging her knees.

"Hello, nipper," said Cooley.

Julie turned her head to watch him pass. She was a topaz angel of a child, mercurial, piquant, thoroughly spoiled. Her skin shone from expensive foods, pure milk, the finest soaps; her clothes were as crisp and fresh and clean as new popcorn.

The maid slid back a glass door opening on the back terrace. "Here's the insurance man, Mr. Hovard."

Hovard sat in a white wrought-iron chair under a grape arbor. The leaves over his head glowed green; pale half dollars from the swimming pool danced on his face. He was a large man with brown hair, wide-set eyes and arched eyebrows.

"Mr. Cooley, is it?"

"That's right." Cooley drew up a chair. "Mr. Hovard, I've looked into this matter, and I'm afraid it's not quite an open-and-shut situation. Especially since it involves your little girl."

"What's Julie got to do with it?"

"Well — after all, she was driving."

"Driving!" Hovard frowned uncertainly.

"She was driving the car when it struck Robert Struve."

"That's utter nonsense!" snapped Hovard.

Cooley nodded judiciously. "Then she was not guiding the car when it struck Robert Struve?"

"I said she wasn't driving! She might have been steering. Playing at steering, that is."

Cooley nodded. "I see...Well, we're not unreasonable, Mr. Hovard—but you must know the terms of your policy."

"Certainly. I'm protected in every way!"

Cooley rapped a booklet on the table. "I don't want to be difficult Mr. Hovard, but the policy provides coverage only while a legally licensed operator is in control of the car."

"Would you care to look at my license?"

Cooley grinned. "I'd like to see your little girl's."

"She has no part in this. I was sitting in the driver's seat—in full control of the car."

"I'm very sorry about this Mr. Hovard," said Cooley. "The question of responsibility seems to hinge on who was in control of the car, you or your daughter. I've spoken to witnesses who agree that your little daughter was steering."

"That's a damned lie!" Hovard was pale and grim.

"That may well be so," Cooley agreed politely, "but appearances seem to indicate otherwise. You'll understand, Mr. Hovard, we can't shoulder responsibility for what might well be criminal negligence."

Hovard slowly began to hunch forward. "Are you suggesting that I am criminally negligent?"

Cooley pulled out his cigarettes with airy unconcern. "If Robert dies—it's possible you'll find yourself prosecuted for manslaughter."

Hovard sank back in his chair. "He's not going to die."

"Who's not going to die, Daddy?" asked Julie from behind him.

"Nobody, dear...Run along now."

Julie disappeared inside the house.

"Cute kid," said Cooley. "Too bad she's mixed up in this business."

Hovard glared. "She doesn't know. I'm not going to let her know."

Cooley nodded, ready to rise. "Well, that's it Mr. Hovard. Sorry I can't give you more cheerful news."

"Just a minute!" said Hovard. "Do you mean to tell me that you're disavowing this policy?"

Cooley shrugged, and rose to his feet. "No hard feelings, Mr. Hovard, but that's the situation."

Hovard said, "I'll tell you one thing—if you think you're going to victimize *me*, you've got another think coming. I'll take you to court!"

"That's up to you, Mr. Hovard." Cooley nodded politely, found his way out.

Darrell Hovard took the telephone with a grimace of distaste. "Darrell Hovard speaking."

"This is Mrs. Struve," said Elsbeth. She was calling from the booth in the hospital waiting room. "I'm Robert's mother."

"Oh yes, Mrs. Struve."

"I was talking to the insurance man, and he tells me that they're not responsible..."

"Of course they're responsible! Don't let them tell you otherwise!"

Elsbeth asked hesitantly, "Don't you think it's a matter *you'd* better straighten out with them? Somebody's got to pay the doctor bills; and I've priced plastic surgery. It's just awful what everything's going to cost."

"Well, Mrs. Struve," said Hovard in a harassed voice, "I don't really see what I can do. I've paid my insurance premiums faithfully. As I see it, the matter's up to the insurance company."

Elsbeth's eyes, already sore from tears, began to throb.

"Just how much do the hospital bills come to, Mrs. Struve?"

"With all the plastic surgery and the care, they say it'll be two or three thousand dollars — and we can't afford it."

"Of course not," said Mr. Hovard hastily. "If I weren't insured, Mrs. Struve, there'd be no question — but now they're trying to pass the buck, and I won't stand for it."

"They say your little girl was driving. They say you're the man I should collect from."

"That's utter nonsense, Mrs. Struve, and you know it as well as I do."

"I think I'd better see an attorney," said Elsbeth.

"You do as you think best, Mrs. Struve."

Chapter II

Elsbeth hired Attorney Albert A. Marschott on a fifty-fifty contingency basis. Marschott visited the hospital, shook Robert's hand, looked under the bandages, and assured Elsbeth that fifty thousand dollars was not an unreasonable sum to ask. He added a safety factor, and came up with a final figure of $75,221; and so filed suit against Darrell Hovard.

Hovard, in turn, filed against the Magna Insurance Company for $86,000. The extra ten thousand was intended to cover such damages as he himself might sustain by fighting the suit. He theorized that it gave him a good bargaining position.

He was right. Harvey Dittle, regional manager for Magna Insurance, reviewed Cooley's report, then called Cooley into his office.

"About this Struve business. The kid was riding a motor-scooter when he was hit?"

"Right."

"He's thirteen, it says here. He couldn't have had an operator's license."

"No. But the cops usually wink at kids on motor-bikes."

Dittle gave Edward Cooley a sour look. "They won't wink if it's costing us eighty-six thousand smackers!" He slapped the papers down on his desk. "Try for a settlement with Mrs. Struve. Explain that she hasn't got much of a case against Hovard. It's a matter of illegalities canceling each other. For instance, maybe Robert ran into the Cadillac — how does she know? Maybe Hovard will get a judgment against her. Then she'll be up a pole."

"I see."

"Sound her on a cash settlement. Don't let her get near her attorney; he'll ask for the moon."

When Cooley approached Elsbeth the second time, he found her at the lowest ebb of her spirits. The hospital was demanding money; there was none to be had. The school term had started — it would have been Robert's first semester at high school. Now he'd have to wait until January. Marschott was confident of success and Elsbeth wanted to believe him, but in her heart she found it impossible. It was as if she had wandered the hospital corridors for years, breathing the antiseptic air, choking back her worry. Fifty thousand dollars? A pipe dream.

She put up small resistance to Edward Cooley, even took a weird comfort in letting him gull her. She put forward argumentative straw men, and made no protest when Cooley knocked them down. Anything to get this over, to get Robert home! A big company like Magna Insurance wouldn't take advantage of her! Of course not, said Cooley. A realistic lawyer would advise her to make a friendly settlement on reasonable terms.

"We'll pay hospital expenses up to now, and another thousand to take care of odds and ends — plastic surgery, stuff like that."

Elsbeth felt a pang of rebellion. "A thousand won't hardly get started!"

"Well," said Cooley, "I think I can talk Dittle into twelve hundred fifty. In fact, I'll put that figure here in the settlement, even if I get fired for it!"

"That's very nice of you," said Elsbeth weakly, and signed where Cooley showed her.

When Elsbeth telephoned Albert Marschott, he found it difficult to control his voice. After a moment he told Mrs. Struve that she was entitled to manage her own life. He said, "Good day," and hung up. Elsbeth felt bleak and lost and lonesome. "What have I done?" she whispered to herself.

The check for $1,250 was deposited in Robert's 'college fund'. Elsbeth had only worked part time during Robert's stay in the hospital, and she was forced to borrow from the $1,250.

Robert finally came home. His face had healed, but Elsbeth had to stifle gasps every time she looked at him. Could this be her Robert, the dear little boy who was all she had? His mouth was drawn over to the side; his left cheek was like a dish of brains. Above the mouth was a low gristly ridge, with black holes for nostrils. The eyebrows had been burnt off, and were growing back in odd angles. The forehead was unmarred; the eyes looked forth bewildered and frantic.

Robert refused to leave the apartment. He closed himself in his room, the shades drawn.

"I'm never going out," he said. "Never again... Everybody looks at me and stares. I'm a freak."

At last Elsbeth said, "Only a coward is afraid of what people think, Robert. The worst kind of coward. A man who runs from danger is wise, but a man who runs from what people think, when he knows he's right, isn't true to himself."

"Okay," said Robert, looking bleakly out the window. "Okay, I'll try it."

He bandaged his face, and went with Elsbeth to the supermarket. No one paid any attention to him, and Robert took courage.

A week later he resumed his paper route. He still bandaged his face, but less elaborately. On the fourth day he met Carr Pendry riding his bike home from high school. Carr signaled urgently. Robert halted and slid from his bike. Carr made a circuit and coasted up.

"Hi," said Robert.

"Hi." Carr's eyes lingered on the bandage. "I heard you were out of the hospital. How do you feel?"

"Okay."

Carr nodded. He was solid and chunky, with a square face, a thatch of golden hair. He said bluntly, "What about my jigger?"

"What about it?" Robert asked, puzzled.

"It's wrecked, isn't it?"

Robert had nothing to say.

"I heard the insurance company made you a big payment," said Carr. "My father says you're responsible for the damage."

Robert looked uneasily up the street. "I'm not going to pay for something I didn't do."

"But you were riding it!" Carr was becoming angry.

"I'm sorry," said Robert. "Mr. Hovard ran into me. I'm not going to pay his damages. Especially when Julie Hovard was driving."

Carr nodded bitterly. "That's what I get, lending my stuff to guys."

"I was delivering your route. It might have been you!"

Carr looked startled. "I never thought of that. I guess I was lucky."

"I guess I wasn't."

Carr leaned forward, peered at the bandage. "Did you get burned pretty bad?"

"Yeah."

Carr came a step forward. "Let's see what it looks like."

"It's nothing special." Robert turned away, preparing to get on his bike.

"Aw, come on."

Robert shook his head. "Wait till I get the plastic surgery."

"When's that?"

"I don't know yet. Pretty soon."

Carr called up the street: "Hey, Grant!"

Grant Hovard sauntered up. He was fifteen, an ungainly beanpole. His head was like his father's, low and round, with soft black hair cut close to the scalp, like a pad of black felt. His eyes were large and bulging.

He propped himself against the trunk of an acacia tree which grew out of the sidewalk strip.

"Hi, Grant," said Robert. He threw his leg over the frame of his bike.

"Just a minute," said Carr.

Robert gripped the handlebars uneasily. Carr was known for sudden recklessness. It was rumored that he beat up his sister Dean in wild tantrums.

Grant Hovard lounged back against the tree. "What's the deal?"

"Robert was just telling me about his accident," said Carr. "What do you think of a guy that ruins another guy's jigger, then won't pay for it?"

Grant shrugged, eyeing Robert sidelong.

"He says Julie ran into him."

"That's silly," said Grant.

Carr's eyes were bright and daring. "He says he's uglier than you are."

"Maybe he is," said Grant. "He'll have to prove it, though."

"Oh, hell," said Robert, feeling the warm blood pulsing under the scars. He pushed Carr away from the front of his bike. "I got to deliver my route."

"Just a minute," said Grant. "You mean to say you're uglier than I am?"

"I don't care one way or the other," said Robert tensely.

Carr laughed mockingly. "We ought to find out, hey Grant?"

"I got a title to defend," said Grant, even though something inside his brain quailed and shrank. "Let's take a look."

Robert tried to ride off, but Grant caught him from behind, under the armpits. The two tripped on the bicycle, fell to the dry grass between street and sidewalk. Carr snatched at the bandage; the adhesive tape tore at the pale pink tissue.

They looked into Robert's face. Carr dropped the bandage as if it were foul. Grant rose to his feet, drew back a step.

Robert felt himself a different person — strong and swift as the wind. He reached out, grabbed the air pump from the clip on Carr's bicycle, and leaped to his feet.

"Look out," muttered Grant.

Carr stumbled. Robert hit him on the ear, then swung at Grant, but Grant skipped away.

Carr tried to struggle up. Robert struck him again, and Carr fell back to his knees. Robert raised his arm, but Grant snatched the pump out of his grasp. Robert rushed at Grant, ran him backwards into the picket fence.

Grant, yelling in alarm and pain, managed to writhe free.

Carr staggered forward. Robert struck with his fist, felt the warm wad of Carr's nose under his knuckles, the spurt of blood. Grant was coming at him with the pump. Robert ran to meet him. Grant shied back and stood panting.

"You better be careful." He raised the air pump. "I'll let you have it."

Robert looked at Carr, who was holding a handkerchief to his nose. For a few seconds there was a peculiar hush. Then Robert went to his bike, got on and rode away.

A block down the street Robert remembered his bandage. He laughed. His face was naked, and it was as if his whole body were naked. He felt immensely powerful. His face was responsible. It gave him a stern and terrible force.

He never wore the bandage again.

In late October he and Elsbeth paid a visit to the county hospital. The 'college fund' had dwindled to an even $800.

Dr. Sunderland inspected Robert's face. "Healing very well. You've got tough tissue there, Robert."

"What about plastic surgery?" asked Elsbeth.

The doctor leaned back in his chair. "Frankly, Mrs. Struve, it's a big job — specialist's work. Not just skin graft, but an entire modeling of the face. I'd suggest that you consult Banbery, in San Francisco. Dr. Felix Banbery. He's the best man in the field."

"Is he expensive?" Elsbeth ventured.

Dr. Sunderland smiled briskly. "Any work of this kind is expensive. You might try the clinic — but of course they're working overtime on emergency cases."

Elsbeth rose to her feet. "Thank you, Dr. Sunderland."

They descended to the county clinic in the basement. The nurse was busy with paper work; it seemed to Elsbeth that she listened with only half an ear.

Elsbeth explained the problem. The nurse looked over Elsbeth's clothes, which were inexpensive but carefully chosen. "You're without means?"

Elsbeth bridled at the nurse's tone. "We're not paupers; we —"

The nurse interrupted, "I can put your name down, but we're full up for two months. Also, you understand that the boy'll be immobilized; he'll have to lie quiet for months."

"But he's starting high school," protested Elsbeth. "Can't the work be done on weekends? Or after school?"

The nurse shook her head. "No ma'am."

Elsbeth gave her name, then she and Robert went home. Robert had never seen her look so old. He wandered restlessly about the room, fingering magazines, the bits of pottery that Elsbeth considered cute: roguish kittens, prancing deer, squirrels, puppies, skunks. Elsbeth said, "I don't know what to do. I just don't know what to do."

"I don't want to go to the hospital."

Elsbeth shook her head. "But you've got to, Robert!" She considered. "If I could get a good job in the city, we'd be near the doctor..."

"I got to deliver my route," said Robert. Elsbeth jumped up and hugged him fiercely, tears burning in her eyes.

The telephone rang. It was Mrs. Agnes Sadko, office manager at Hegenbels. She sounded very cool. "You'll be in for sure tomorrow?"

"I surely will, Mrs. Sadko."

"Very well, Mrs. Struve. We'll see you in the morning."

The next day Mrs. Sadko took Elsbeth aside. "Now, Mrs. Struve, I know you've been under a great strain, and we all feel the utmost sympathy. But the work here at the office is suffering. We're going to have to make some kind of arrangement."

Elsbeth's heart came into her mouth. "Arrangement?"

Mrs. Sadko cleared her throat. "We've got to get the work done, that's what we're here for... We're getting behind."

Elsbeth heaved a great sigh. "I think the worst of it's over. Robert's well now. We've decided to wait before going into plastic surgery."

Mrs. Sadko nodded brusquely. "Well, I'm glad to hear you're getting straightened out."

Chapter III

In January, Robert started high school. Elsbeth had concocted a brave fiction that nothing really had happened; that Robert was like the other boys.

If Robert was not precisely cheerful, at least he did not mope. He fitted into school routine without effort, applying himself to his homework with a remarkable intensity. He never had been a confiding boy; now he closed tighter than a clam.

During his second semester, and to Elsbeth's surprise and vague disapproval, Robert decided to play football. He wore a wire mask and practiced with the same intensity he gave his homework. It was a foregone conclusion that he'd make the Junior Varsity.

The JV quarterbacks were Alonzo Sanguarez, a Mexican in his junior year, and Carr Pendry, a low sophomore and one football season ahead of Robert. Alonzo was fast and a good ball-handler; Carr was clever, brash and confident. The coach rated them about even.

Carr started the first game of the season, against Calmetta. After two minutes it was clear that Carr was not planning to make Robert look good. During the whole of the first quarter he handed off either to left halfback Ron Caffrey, fullback Jim Smith, or threw passes. Robert tackled, applied his blocks, ran interference.

The game was not going well for San Giorgio. Calmetta was strong and tough. They intercepted one of Carr's passes and ran it to a touchdown. In the early second quarter Carr called on Robert for a line buck. Robert had been waiting for this moment. The ball touched his hands, and it was like a fuse. Calmetta arms and shoulders seemed to melt in front of him. He was running free. Touchdown.

Robert throbbed with a grim joy, pleased but not surprised. Carr set out to prove that Robert had been lucky, and handed off to him six times in a row. Four times Robert broke loose for long gains; the last time he scored a touchdown.

Carr stopped handing off to Robert, sought rather to overshadow him by a series of brilliant passes, but twice his passes were intercepted, and one more went for a Calmetta touchdown.

At half time the coach gave Robert a slap on the back. "Good work, kid. Just don't kill anybody out there."

During the third quarter, Alonzo Sanguarez came into the game as quarterback. Robert scored two more touchdowns.

The team had a successful season, winning all but the game against Paytonville. Elsbeth's initial disapproval became delight and pride. She suggested a party for the football team, but Robert vetoed the idea with a curtness that bewildered her.

Plastic surgery was still a project for the middle future. The clinic never called about an appointment, and Elsbeth put off making inquiries. She must not make a nuisance of herself.

The football season passed, then Christmas, and the spring semester drew to a close. Elsbeth resolved to do something about Robert's face during vacation. But in early June Robert was offered a summer job as stock-boy at Hegenbels, which he accepted. Elsbeth was uncomfortable but vaguely relieved. After all, they really didn't have the money.

Summer came to an end; Robert began his fourth semester. His grades continued excellent; he made the California Scholarship Federation, and the principal discussed scholarships with him. Robert was interested but vague; he had no clear picture of his future. And then there was always the plastic surgery that sooner or later had to be undergone. He played halfback on the Varsity football team. Carr was second-string quarterback after Harold Garrow. The line was weak, competition tough. San Giorgio had a poor year, winning two, losing six.

Another Christmas, another spring semester, another Commencement. Grant Hovard graduated. Summer passed.

The fall semester began. Grant Hovard went down to Stanford for pre-med training. Carr was a senior; his pretty sister, Dean, a freshman. Julie was starting eighth grade.

Another football season came and went. San Giorgio tied Paytonville for league championship, and Robert achieved a certain grim reputation around the county. He was known as 'The Face', or 'No-Face'; sometimes as 'The Masked Marvel'; and once, in a sports column, as the "Red Wolf of San Giorgio — when he doesn't blast 'em out of his way, he scares 'em stiff."

The prettiest girl in school was Cathy McDermott, a sophomore. She was slender, beautifully formed. Her hair was the color of black coffee and hung past her shoulders; she had dark poetic eyes. Her father was Ralph McDermott, president and chief stockholder of the San Giorgio Building and Loan Association. They lived on Jamaica Terrace next to the Pendrys.

Robert took his courage in hand one day and asked her for a date. His voice trembled with nervousness. In a voice equally nervous, she told him thanks but she was all dated up. Later he happened to be walking behind her in the hall while she told her friend Lucia Small about it.

"And what did you say?" Lucia asked.

"What could I say? I told him I was dated ten years ahead."

They saw Robert, and fell silent.

"Hi," said Robert.

"Hi," said Cathy in a subdued voice.

Carr Pendry came up, gave Cathy a casual spank with his books. "What's going on here? Robert trying to make time with my girl?"

"More or less," said Robert. "Mostly less."

He walked away.

Carr's fraternity was Rho Sigma Rho, a trifle more exclusive than Beta Zeta. The sororities were Nu Alpha Tau (or the NATs) and Tri-Gamma — known as 'Lucky Thirteen', because membership was restricted to this number. Freshmen were pledged on 'tag day' just before commencement, with 'hell week' in September and initiation in October of the semester following.

Julie Hovard raised havoc with this system. She started high school at the beginning of Robert's last year; it was certain that she'd be pledged at the end of the year, either by the NATs or Tri-Gamma. She wanted to go Tri-Gamma. Cathy McDermott, her best friend, was a Tri-Gamma pledge, along with Dean Pendry and Lucia Small, old Judge Small's daughter.

Cathy, Dean, and Lucia were all sophomores, a year or two older than Julie. Dean had auburn hair, a voluptuous figure, a lovely pale complexion. She was fifteen but looked older; she went out with boys from the junior college.

Lucia had an entirely different outlook on life. She was tall, aristocratic, alert. She had dark hair, sharp eyes, a high-bridged nose. She spoke of a career in psychology and planned to go on to Radcliffe.

During the summer, Marian Scheib moved south to Pasadena, leaving a vacancy in Tri-Gamma. Julie decided to take advantage of the situation. She told one of the NATs that she'd probably go Tri-Gamma, and hinted to Anne Bresdick, president of Tri-Gamma, that she'd already been asked to go NAT.

A furious four-day battle was waged around Julie, and as a result she was immediately pledged by Tri-Gamma.

Julie was now almost fourteen, the very breath of youth and vitality. She chattered and laughed and played games; she looked as if she found everything in the world a delightful surprise. She flirted widely, gaily, innocently. She sat across from Robert in study hall, and he found it impossible to take his eyes off her. Julie flirted with him as readily as anyone else; sometimes Robert thought even more so… But no, it couldn't be… And yet — it was football season. Robert was a celebrity. He was declared the most effective halfback in San Giorgio history.

"— astonishing the change that comes over him," declared Bing Burns, sports editor of the *Herald-Republican.* "The difference between a quiet, retiring lad and a ravening tiger seems to be only a football uniform. Because Robert Struve just won't be stopped. The harder the going, the harder goes Robert. It's not that he's big, or heavy, or fast, he just refuses to say no…"

Already he'd had offers from Southern California, the College of the Pacific in Stockton and the University of Maryland.

On September 27 Robert celebrated his eighteenth birthday. Elsbeth baked a small cake, roasted a chicken, and bought a bottle of sauterne. They ate by candlelight, and in honor of the occasion Robert drank a glass of wine.

Elsbeth looked at him fondly across the table. He had a well-knit husky frame, something under six feet. His hair was cropped short. Elsbeth thought if only his face were mended, he'd be such a nice-looking boy... As soon as he graduated — plastic surgery.

After dinner Robert went off to his room. For once he was not studying. He was examining the letter Barbara Fisher had passed him earlier in the day. Barbara was an important girl around school. She had an insolent triangle of a face, loose flaxen ringlets, and looked like a fashion model. She was Tri-Gamma, one of the Lucky Thirteen.

The letter was brief, tantalizing:

Dear Robert,

Lucky 13 rips the lid off! You are invited to attend the initiation of our four pledges: Lucia Small, Cathy McDermott, Julie Hovard, and Dean Pendry. Need we say, this is secret? This Saturday night, at the Martin house, out on Vinedale Road. You know where it is. If you can't come, let me know.

The idea fascinated Robert. He had visions of girl-rites — fair young bodies — madness — abandon... Julie Hovard... Something clenched in his stomach. He wouldn't go. Why did they seek him out?

The next day he waited beside Barbara Fisher's locker until she came. "What's going on at this affair?" he asked her.

She glanced at him sidelong, then looked away into her locker. "Just the usual stuff. An initiation. There'll be a party afterwards. Don't you want to come?"

"No," said Robert, "not especially."

"The rest of the team's invited, too," said Barbara.

"Oh," said Robert. He had thought they wanted him there alone.

She turned him another swift glance. "Are you coming?"

"I don't know for sure."

"What's the matter?" she asked. "Scared?"

"Okay," said Robert woodenly. "I'll come."

"Sure now?" said Barbara.

"Yes," said Robert.

She nodded casually and went off down the hall.

When Robert went to bed that night, the vision persisted. He fell asleep to a dream that he was dancing with Julie in the gymnasium, at one of the dances to which he never went. The music stopped; Julie turned up her face, gave him a look of heart-stopping significance. He reached out his arms, but she laughed and skipped off. Then she ran back, caught his hands, led him outside to a big sedan parked under the trees. He opened the door, she got in; he got in after her... Robert awoke.

He lay with his heart pounding. He wanted to go back to sleep, back to the dream... He reached up, felt his face. The coils felt hard, smooth as sausages. "I wonder," whispered Robert to himself. "I wonder..."

The next day, remembering the dream, he watched Julie in the study hall. He studied the swell of her young hips, the jaunty little breasts. Somehow he felt closer to her. She looked up, saw him watching her, made a friendly grimace, half-nod, half-wrinkling of her nose, went back to work.

Robert bent over his books. What went on in her mind? Did she realize that she was responsible for his face? She seemed perfectly unconscious... Had she forgotten? He looked up again and found her watching him. She wasn't smiling; she was chewing thoughtfully on her pencil. He wondered if he dared ask for a date...

Chapter IV

The Saturday of the initiation was an open date on the football schedule; there was no game.

Elsbeth came home from work and went straight to bed, and Robert got his own dinner. When it came time for him to leave, Elsbeth was asleep.

Robert went over to Bob Goble's house and found Bob in his car, a stripped-down V-8. With him were the two big tackles: John Strykos and Babe Bazzari. They sat in the front seat passing a jug of sherry back and forth; in the back were two more jugs.

The three hailed Robert as a long-lost brother, and bundled him into the back seat. Robert was pleased and embarrassed.

Bob started to pass the jug back to Robert. John Strykos said, "Hell, give Robert a full one; he's a big boy."

Robert murmured something deprecatory. But he opened a jug, took a pull. The stuff was pretty good; it had an olive-and-nut flavor and puckered the inside of his mouth.

"Don't suppose the coach would go much for this," said Robert humorously.

"This stuff is good for a guy," said Bazzari. "It puts steam in his pipes."

"Yeah," said Robert, and took another swallow.

"Hey," said John, "it's eight o'clock. Let's get the show on the road."

"C'mon, c'mon," agreed Bazzari, "let's get going!"

The Martin house on Vinedale Road had been vacant for eight months. It was an old-fashioned barn of a place, brown-shingled, half-submerged in ivy. The front door opened into an echoing living room, paneled with dark wood; an arch connected to the dining room, with the kitchen beyond. A hall gave access to two bedrooms and a bathroom. A big old house full of ghosts and faint sounds. A dozen redwood trees crowded the sky; the ground was dark and sour and dank. Hamilton Duncan, the present owner, had taken the house in satisfaction of a debt; now he found it impossible to get rid of.

Dorothy Duncan was Tri-Gamma. Her father had given her permission to use the house for the initiation. "Just be careful," he warned her. "Don't light any fires. And don't raise too much hell, or you'll have the sheriff out."

At two o'clock Saturday afternoon, eight of the nine members — all except Barbara Fisher — arrived at the Martin house; they opened the doors and windows, ran dust mops over the hardwood floors, laid out the secret properties of the order.

There was only a sagging sofa and a few rickety chairs in the house; the girls arranged them in the living room, and spread blankets on the floor alongside the walls.

At four o'clock Barbara Fisher arrived with the four pledges and refreshments, which the pledges had been required to buy. The pledges were taken to the porch, blindfolded, led through the living room into one of the bedrooms; here they were allowed to remove their blindfolds. On the floor they found a pile of burlap sacks and a pair of scissors.

"Okay kids," said Anne Bresdick. "There's your clothes for the day."

"What are we supposed to do?" Julie asked.

"Take off your outer clothes, shoes and socks. The rest of it's up to you. There's two sacks apiece."

Cutting appropriate holes, the girls made themselves costumes, using one sack for a skirt, the other as a blouse.

At four-thirty Barbara Fisher and Anne Bresdick came into the bedroom. Again they blindfolded the pledges and took them into the living room, lined them up with their backs to the sacred table.

The pledges were sprayed with purifying fluids. Anne Bresdick, president of the order, addressed them in a solemn voice, and the rites began.

At six o'clock they were allowed to remove the blindfolds, and now came the candle-lighting ceremony. The room was dark: there was only the glow of a single big green candle. Each member held her own candle; the pledges were given new ones.

"Each of these thirteen candles represents one of us," said Anne. "They'll be with us all our lives. They're our sacred candles, and during the great moments of our lives we light them.

"Each of you may now light your candle from the sacred green candle of the order."

Each of the four pledges lighted her candle, faces solemn and pale. The nine members approached the table and did likewise.

The pledges were next sworn; they bound themselves never to reveal the secrets of the order, to stand by their sisters through thick and thin.

Then came a ceremony with faintly erotic overtones. Each pledge lowered her burlap skirt and her step-ins and stood with her face to the wall. Lucia Small made restless rebellious sounds. Dean Pendry was flushed, excited. Cathy McDermott stood rigid as a statue. Julie Hovard waited.

"A Tri-Gamma now is a Tri-Gamma always," Anne Bresdick chanted. And the initiates chanted back, "A Tri-Gamma now is a Tri-Gamma always."

"A Tri-Gamma now is a Tri-Gamma always," sang Anne, and the initiates sang dolefully back — over and over again, interrupting the liturgy with squeals as their buttocks were touched with black ink, pricked three times with a needle: tattooed.

"Wherever you go, you now are proven Tri-Gammas!"

"Must I show my bottom every time somebody asks if I'm Tri-Gamma?" growled Lucia, as they pulled up their garments.

Each pledge wrote her name on a gummed slip, sealed it with a drop of blood, and pasted it over the name of the girl whose place she was stepping into. The candles were blown out; the initiates were congratulated at having passed the first phase of the ordeal.

"First phase?" cried Julie. "Golly, do we have to go through more stuff?"

"You're all on probation until exactly one week from tonight — and then you become full members."

Cathy McDermott rubbed her new tattoo. "It itches... There's nothing more like that, is there?"

"No questions," Anne said sternly.

It was now 7:30; the boys would be arriving at any minute. The pledges were instructed in their duties; the members retired to the kitchen for Cokes.

At eight o'clock two cars arrived almost simultaneously. The boys piled out, climbed noisily up on the porch.

Julie opened the door with a flourish, stepped back, knelt submissively as the boys marched in. Cathy, Lucia Small, and Dean Pendry performed low curtsies, ushered them into the room.

Anne, looking through a crack in the door, whispered, "They've been drinking." She giggled.

Beaming aimlessly in all directions, Robert steered himself into a chair in the corner. He was still clasping his jug of sherry; to display his innate deviltry, he lifted the bottle and took a gulp.

"Robert," said Julie, "you'd better stop that, you'll be so pie-eyed you won't know what you're doing."

"I know what I'm doing," said Robert, and indeed he did; never before had he felt so astonishingly rational. He reached an arm out for Julie, who sprang back.

"Easy, Robert," called Bob Goble. "That's for later."

The nine members made their entry. The pledges stood to the side, bowing deeply. Anne turned, flourished her arm in a regal gesture. "Slaves! Serve the ceremonial banquet!"

"Oh boy! We eat!" cried Babe Bazzari. "Whatcha got?"

The pledges came crouching in with sandwiches, potato chips, Cokes and a case of canned beer.

"In case somebody was thirsty," said Barbara, slanting a look at Robert.

"A noble sentiment!" said Omar Williams, the flashy left halfback. Omar was a great admirer of Robert's; he felt in Robert something of the old crusader spirit, a ruthless hell-for-leather recklessness.

Robert, totally unaware that anyone respected or admired him, sat quietly eating his second sandwich, and drinking beer.

Somebody asked what was the program for the evening; Barbara asked provocatively what they wanted to do.

"Hell," said John Strykos, "this here is an initiation; we figure you girls want to be initiated."

"You forget," said Anne with dignity, "that this is a serious occasion — a Tri-Gamma initiation."

"Let's drink to the initiation and hope it takes."

"If you like. Make mine a Coke."

"Aw, come on. Take a slug of the sherry. It's good!"

"No, sir. You drink it if you like it so much."

Robert, in the corner, took a drink; and presently realized it had been a mistake. His head was spinning; the room was bright and dim at the same time. Maybe if he walked around — or better, rested a moment or so in the other room… He rose to his feet, staggered out through the hall and into one of the bedrooms. Somebody ran after him: one of the girls. He never knew who it was.

"It's not in here, Robert — in fact, there isn't any. Water's shut off. You'll have to go outside."

"Just want to rest," Robert mumbled in a thick voice. "Just want to sit down a few minutes."

"Oh. Well, there's nothing but the floor… If you want to go outside, that door opens on the porch."

"Thanks." Robert sat down hard, his back to the wall, his head down over his chest.

From the living room came a jumble of sound: voices, laughing, music from a portable radio, the shuffle of feet dancing…

Anne said, "Now we're going to have a command performance — a real talent show! Tri-Gamma has just acquired four lovely young ladies, and tonight — just for tonight — they'll do anything you ask them."

"Anything, eh?" John Strykos said.

"Within certain limits. After all, this is the Tri-Gamma."

"Okay, let's see them dance the cancan."

Julie, Cathy, Lucia, and Dean danced their interpretation of the cancan.

"Now they can do a strip-tease."

"I don't know how," said Julie simply.

"There's nothing to it. You just take off your clothes."

"That's outside the limits," said Dorothy Duncan.

"Well, they can do a strip-tease without taking their clothes off. Just pretending."

"Well — I suppose it's part of their education."

The four girls went awkwardly through the motions of throwing off their clothes.

"Now," said Bob Goble, "they've all got to go in the other room and kiss Robert."

Robert was feeling better. He was drawing deep breaths; his head felt securely anchored on his neck. Out in the living room he heard a great laugh, some voices raised in protest, other voices arguing. He heard footsteps in the hall; the door opened. Cathy McDermott came in holding a candle, followed by Dean Pendry and Lucia Small. Julie, opening cans of beer in the kitchen, had been delayed. Robert closed his eyes and pretended to be asleep.

There was silence. He felt their eyes on his face. The blood began to pound in his scars. He heard Cathy whisper, "He's out. Dead drunk."

Robert breathed a little harder, and fought the temptation to open his eyes.

"Listen," said Lucia in a whisper, "let's go back and say we kissed him. We don't need to do it."

"Gaaa," said Dean. "I just couldn't take it."

"I couldn't, either," said Cathy. "Anybody but Robert. Simply anybody."

Fires were lighting inside Robert's brain; he wanted to jump up, to smite, curse, hurt...

Cathy said anxiously, "He is drunk, isn't he? I thought I saw his face move."

"Hurry," said Lucia. "Here, rub lipstick on him."

"You do it," giggled Cathy. "I don't want to touch him."

"Oh, we don't need the lipstick. Let's go back. And remember, we've got to make faces, and act disgusted..."

He heard them leave the room, and he jumped to his feet, pressed back against the wall, staring into the blackness. Something hard and hot began to move up into his brain. He clenched and unclenched his hands, feeling the muscles twist in his arms.

It was all so clear, suddenly. He'd sensed it a long time — but now it was like crystal. They hated him. And he hated them...

Julie came into the room holding a candle. She looked at him and grinned sheepishly. "They told me you were asleep."

"I'm not asleep."

She came a hesitant step nearer. "I'm supposed to kiss you."

Robert took a great breath; all the oxygen in the world entered his lungs, his blood-stream; it rang up into his head. The dream... The dream... He remembered the dream...

"Julie, put down the candle."

"Oh — Robert — let's not make this too involved."

A bitter voice muttered inside Robert's brain... Remember the dream? sang another voice. The blood pumped in his ears. He stepped forward. Julie said, "Robert, look out! The candle!"

Robert spoke in a thick, rapid voice. "What are you staring at?"

"You, of course." She laughed nervously.

"Don't like my face, do you?"

"Well — it could be improved."

"Yeah. I guess so."

"Oh Robert, you shouldn't talk like that. I've got to kiss you... stand still..."

In the living room John Strykos noticed that Julie had been gone quite a while. "Robert seems to be making the grade."

Bob Goble, looking out the window, said, "Cripes! It's the law!"

A car with glaring red searchlights had quietly pulled into the driveway.

"Ditch the sherry," said John. "Hide the beer."

"Let's get outa here," said Babe Bazzari.

"Is this all of you?" Sheriff Hartmann asked Dorothy Duncan.

"This is all," she said with great dignity. "We're not doing anything wrong; this is my father's house."

"All but Robert and Julie," said Barbara.

The sheriff sent a man into the house to check.

Three or four minutes later the deputy called the sheriff to the house. After a minute he came out. He seemed excited. "Okay. Give your names to the deputy and go home, do you hear? Go home!"

"But what about Julie — and Robert?"

The sheriff smiled sourly. "You kids go home."

*

The hearing was conducted at a closed session of the juvenile court. Darrell Hovard had signed the complaint in his first flood of fury, with the image of Julie's tear-swollen face stamped on his mind.

Julie, after a medical examination and a good cry, seemed to have suffered small physical damage and certainly less psychological trauma than either Darrell or Margaret Hovard.

Judge Theresa Kleiderle, presiding at juvenile court, remanded Robert to the Las Lomas Detention Home until his majority.

"You got off lucky, kid," said the beetle-browed deputy sheriff. "In this state it's the gas chamber. Yeah, you got off easy."

"Yeah," said Robert.

Elsbeth had not been able to visit him in the jail; the fabric of her life had suddenly separated into shreds and ravels. She gave in to a fit of hysterics and was hustled to emergency hospital. During treatment a swelling on her lower abdomen was noticed, which under examination proved to be a tumor. Luckily Elsbeth was covered by health insurance sponsored by Hegenbels, and there would be no medical bills.

The deputy took Robert to see his mother before they set out for Las Lomas. Robert was aghast to find her so drawn and pale, such a pitiful bundle of bones under the white coverlet.

"Be a good boy, Robert. Always remember..."

"Yes, Mother," said Robert. He and the deputy caught the afternoon train.

At school there was a clatter of talk. Julie dealt with the excited questions calmly enough. She said that Robert had merely tried to get fresh; that she had her hands full holding him off. She seemed so casual and unruffled that the event was no more than a nine-day wonder.

By Christmas Robert was hardly more than a name; at the end of the school year he was almost forgotten.

Julie was elected vice-president of the sophomore class; she began going steady with Dale Hemet.

If anything troubled her easygoing young mind, it was a wisp of recollection from the far past. She asked Darrell Hovard about it. "Daddy — do you remember a long time ago? I was steering the car. We ran into something and you wouldn't let me look..."

Darrell Hovard put down his newspaper.

"Did we run into Robert then?"

Hovard made a gruff sound in his throat, and nodded.

"Is that why he has a scarred face?"

Darrell Hovard uttered a genial laugh. "Well, there was an accident. Robert was as much to blame as we were."

"But I was driving?"

"You had your hand on the wheel."

Julie sat trying to remember. Little by little, the moment came back. She felt the tingle of excitement, peering over the dash, her arms up, holding the wheel. She saw the red scooter, the blue shirt — and ahead the stone pillars of Jamaica Arch. Rather than take the chance of scratching her daddy's car, she had cut close to the boy. Close, close. A clatter and a thump, and suddenly her daddy was taking the wheel, and holding her head down.

That evening Julie and Cathy McDermott walked down to the public library, to get reference books for an English theme. Julie, rummaging around the shelves, noticed the bound files of the San Giorgio *Herald-Republican*. She stopped short. *It was the forty-one Cadillac,* she thought. *That means it must have been before forty-six, that's when we got the new one... When I was taking piano lessons from Mrs. McKinley Daddy used to meet me and I'd steer part of the way home; that was when I was eight. In nineteen forty-four. It must be nineteen forty-four, at the end of summer.*

She took the second volume for 1944 to a desk. In the issue for July 17, on page 2, she found an article and a picture of Robert Struve, reproduced from a portrait Elsbeth had had taken the year before.

Julie studied the photograph. Her face was quiet, her forehead clear; it would have been impossible to divine her thoughts.

The Las Lomas Detention Home for Boys was a new institution, not six months old. There was no overt restraint, no bars. The dormitories were large and bright; the commissary was more like a cafeteria than a mess hall. The slogan was 'Rehabilitation, not Recrimination'; great stress was put on vocational training; the staff included two psychiatrists and a number of motherly matrons.

Robert made no trouble. Mrs. Fador, the matron in charge of his dormitory, considered him a model inmate. But there was something about Robert that made her uneasy.

One day, while talking to Dr. O'Brien, the head psychologist, she mentioned Robert. "He's like a great brooding hole into nowhere," she told O'Brien.

"Come, come," Dr. O'Brien said, smiling. "You're getting intuitive in your old age."

"No," she insisted.

"Let's see... He's the boy with the horrible face. Let's take a look at his background." Dr. O'Brien went to the files, pulled out the folder tabbed 'Robert Struve', read in silence. "Hmmph," he said, pinching his chin, "it seems a shame to let a kid go through life with a face like that."

"At San Quentin," said Mrs. Fador, "they do plastic surgery on the inmates all the time."

The psychiatrist sighed. "This isn't San Quentin... We just don't have the facilities."

"Sacramento's only thirty miles away."

The psychiatrist picked up the phone and called the director.

The next day Mrs. Fador brought Robert into the psychiatrist's office. She had her arm around his shoulders. "Robert's just had some bad news. Some very bad news."

"What's the trouble?" Dr. O'Brien asked. He was young; he had not yet learned to insulate himself from his work.

"My mother just died," said Robert.

"Oh... I'm sorry Robert."

Robert nodded, blinking.

The psychiatrist cocked a professional eye. "Well, Robert — I've got some good news for you. It doesn't balance your bad news. But it'll help."

"What's that?"

"I've made arrangements for you to undergo plastic surgery."

Robert stood utterly still. His voice was colorless, uninterested; as if the psychiatrist had offered him a cigarette. "No thanks... I got by pretty well before. I guess I can again."

The psychiatrist nodded with easy nonchalance to match Robert's. "Well, just as you like. Think it over."

"Is that all?" asked Robert.

"That's all."

Robert left the office. Mrs. Fador showed concern and bewilderment. "I can't understand! You'd think he'd jump at the chance."

"Give him time," said the psychiatrist.

And the next day Robert asked to see him.

"Hello Robert. Have a seat."

Robert sat down. "Smoke?" asked the psychiatrist.

"No... I don't smoke." He hesitated, then took the plunge. "Yesterday you said — is that offer still open?"

"Sure thing."

Robert seemed to be consulting a set of mental memoranda. "How long will it take?"

"I don't know. Probably a year or more."

"But it'll be done before I get out?"

"I should think so."

"Can I look like anyone I want? I mean, can I choose the kind of face I want?"

O'Brien smiled. "Within limits. No one can alter the shape of the skull or the angle of your jaw."

"But my nose — my face..."

"All I can say for sure, Robert, is that you'll never recognize yourself in a year's time."

"Yes," said Robert, "that's the main thing."

The psychiatrist, loading his pipe, looked curiously at Robert. "You're all alone in the world now, eh, Robert?"

"That's right."

"What do you plan to do when you get out?"

"I'm not sure. When do I start plastic surgery?"

"Next Thursday."

Robert nodded. "Thanks very much." He held out his hand.

O'Brien rose to his feet, shook Robert's hand with sudden humbleness. "Until Thursday, Robert."

Robert left his office, and the psychiatrist went to the window, watched him cross the square toward the dormitory. Robert walked with a stride at once taut and strong, with purpose and direction.

The psychiatrist turned back to his desk.

"I wonder about that boy," he mused. "I wonder what he's got on his mind…"

Chapter V

San Giorgio boomed in the years of the Korean War: new houses, new stores, new schools. Hegenbels tore down the old Tatley Building, constructed a four-story annex; Safeway built a huge new unit out on the Sonoma Highway; the Bank of America moved into new quarters beside the San Giorgio Building and Loan Association. But in spite of the new houses, new roads, new schools, there always seemed to be more people, more cars, more children.

Among the institutions suffering from over-crowding was the San Giorgio Country Club. The bar filled up with strangers; the golf course became impossible.

A group led by Pelton Pendry, William Cloverbolt and Darrell Hovard resigned, and formed the Mountainview Country Club Corporation. They made membership contingent upon ownership of stock, which they sold with immense discretion.

Darrell Hovard served as chairman of the Planning Committee. He negotiated for and bought three hundred acres in the hills west of San Giorgio.

This was 1952, the year of Julie's graduation from high school. July twenty-second was Julie's seventeenth birthday. On the twenty-first, she came home with her father to find Jamaica Terrace heavy with parked cars, the Hovard house tied up with blue and gold bunting like a Christmas package, and a big sign reading 'Happy Birthday, Julie' staked into the lawn.

Julie hugged and kissed her father, jumped out of the car and ran for the house. She was wearing tan shorts, a white T-shirt and moccasins. Her face was dirty, her hair was blown, but Julie didn't care.

She ran into the house; her guests yelled, "Happy Birthday," and then fell silent. A new dark-red Ford convertible occupied the center of the living room. A streamer read, 'Happy Birthday Julie'.

Julie went into transports of joy.

The party moved to the back terrace, while laborers took out two French windows, laid planks and rolled the convertible into the street. On the terrace were tubs of fried chicken and French-fried potatoes, racks of hamburgers, Cokes and orange pop.

Grant Hovard and Carr Pendry were the oldest guests present. Grant, a tall young man with a long nose and a saturnine expression, was home from Johns Hopkins. Carr had just been graduated in economics from Harvard, and talked about going into politics. He still had a crush on Cathy McDermott, now starting her sophomore year at Cal. Carr was blond and dynamic, blocky. He spoke in a ringing staccato as he analyzed the mistakes of men in office, usually finishing up with the prediction, "Right now, things are going to hell. I'll get in at the right time. I'll do my damnedest to lead the reaction, and if I'm lucky, I'll make political hay. I'm gunning, I tell you. I'm gunning, and I'll make it. Lord knows I've got more under my hat than the chucklehead we just booted out."

If Cathy had heard the line once, she had heard it twenty times, and it bored her. But she went out with him, resisting his ardent wooing, making him bring her home early. She kissed him only when she absolutely had to. Cathy had changed very little from her high-school days.

At Julie's birthday party Carr and Grant Hovard drank beer, and later in the evening, highballs. Carr wanted to take Cathy for a ride. Cathy looked meaningfully at Julie, and Julie said that Cathy was staying the night.

At midnight the guests were gone, all except Cathy and Lucia Small. Julie, Cathy and Lucia went out to look at the car; then Julie ran back for the keys.

"Where are you going?" asked Darrell Hovard crossly. The noise of the party had raveled his nerves.

"I'm taking Lucia home, Daddy. I want to try out my new car."

"I want to show you something first." He lumbered out to the street, with Julie following. Cathy and Lucia were talking to Carr, who had stepped across the lawn from the Pendry house next-door.

"Get in," said Hovard.

Julie jumped into the driver's seat.

"Put your hand under here." Julie reached under the dashboard. "What do you feel?"

Julie said, "It's something cold and hard."

"It's a gun," said Hovard. "A .32 automatic. It's loaded. Don't ever touch it unless you need it. Don't show it to anybody." He turned to Cathy and Lucia and Carr. "And none of you mention it around — please."

Julie was properly impressed. "Thanks very much, Daddy."

She eased the convertible down the driveway, out onto Jamaica Terrace. Cathy sat in the middle, with Lucia on the outside. As she approached the arch a light came winking and twisting up the road.

Julie slammed on the brakes.

"What's wrong?" cried Lucia. "What's the trouble?"

Julie said nothing. She coasted until the boy on the bicycle passed them, then slowly accelerated.

"Why did you do that?" asked Cathy.

"I just wanted to make sure he got through the arch."

A quarter mile down the road Julie said, "Remember Robert Struve?"

Cathy looked sidewise at Julie. "What about him?"

"I just happened to think that he must be out of reform school by this time."

Cathy calculated in her head. "He was two classes ahead of me... That would make him about twenty-one. I guess he's out."

"I wonder what he's doing?"

"You talk as if you're interested," remarked Lucia.

"I am — to a certain extent."

Lucia shuddered. "I never could stand the sight of Robert..."

They turned into the side road leading out to the Turrets, the tremendous Victorian mansion where Lucia lived with her father, deaf old Judge Small.

The moon hung big and white over the dark ridge to the west. As they neared the house the ridge bulked higher and blotted out the moon; they drove in under the trees and the night was dark.

At the top of the northeast tower a light glowed; here sat Judge Small, slowly scratching out a book on the origins of common law.

Lucia reluctantly got out of the car. "Why don't you come in? I'll fix some hot chocolate…"

Julie and Cathy both thought they'd better get home; Lucia made them both uneasy. A year at Radcliffe had hardly mellowed her; if anything she was more critical and astringent than she had ever been. Her aristocratic good looks had become merely austere.

They said good night. Julie backed around, drove away from the Turrets, out from under the trees. The moon rose behind the ridge; Julie and Cathy drove back to San Giorgio in perfect companionship.

"Tell me about Dean," said Julie.

This was the scandal of the moment. Dean Pendry had gone to Cal one semester, then had eloped with a musician — a jazz piano player. The Pendrys were putting a good public face on the situation, but turmoil raged in the family circle.

Cathy said, "I didn't see much of Dean last year; she was in a different house: Pi Phi. I met the piano player — in fact, I went out on a double-date with them."

"What's he like?"

Cathy shrugged. "He's pretty young — about Carr's age. He's dark, rather good-looking… I think Dean fell in love with his music, as much as anything."

Julie grinned. "Carr doesn't talk much about it."

Cathy laughed — a secret, delighted laugh. "He's furious. The family won't have anything to do with the new son-in-law."

"What's their name?"

"Mmm… Let's see. Bravonette — no, Bavonette. George Bavonette."

"It's a pretty name."

"The marriage won't last," said Cathy. She leaned back against the seat and sighed. "Just protect me from Carr… He wants me to marry him now, and make some kind of European tour with him."

"Are you going to?"

"Heaven forbid!"

Julie, before going home, went for a lonely drive down the highway… She whistled softly through her teeth, a slow, sad song…

Why wasn't she happier? Julie — whom everyone thought the very definition of light-hearted gaiety! "Oh, fiddle!" said Julie, turning on the radio.

Only after she had gone to bed, and lay looking up into the darkness, did the source of the mood expose itself.

It was Time, the passing of seasons.

Time was making them older, ending their youth. A golden holiday was coming to an end.

Suddenly she had grown out of childhood; she was starting college; she was a young woman, with the responsibilities and privileges of maturity. Soon would come the great choices, the decisions shaping the rest of her life.

Dean Pendry had already made her choice. Silly little fool. Dean had always been boy-crazy; there always had been talk about Dean's disinclination to say no. Dean was the black sheep of the Pendry family, and Carr made no secret of his disapproval. Carr... Julie smiled a little. Blond eager-beaver. Julie thought of him as a husband, and made a wry face in the dark... She tried to picture her own husband, to piece him out of all the individual bits and fragments of requirements. Only the most shadowy figure emerged — a frame of mind rather than a man. He would be someone quiet and sure; a man of integrity and dedication. She would go anywhere with him: explore the Amazon, cross the Gobi Desert in a jeep...

Finally she fell asleep.

Julie was rushed by every sorority on the campus, but pledged Delta Rho Beta, Cathy's house.

In October, Julie and Cathy visited Dean in San Francisco. They arrived about one o'clock, and it was apparent that Dean had only just arisen, for she still wore her bathrobe. Her soft chestnut hair was cut in that shaggy long-short style popularized by Italian cinema stars.

Dean seemed older; certainly her body was riper. She always had had a butter-and-honey figure, and now, while she looked no heavier, she seemed somehow — well, lush.

She was delighted to see Cathy and Julie, but she looked hopelessly around the apartment thinking to herself, *What a mess*! Newspapers littered the floor, ash-trays were full, the end table beside the couch supported five punctured beer cans. Records and record covers were everywhere. Half of one wall was given to gray-painted orange crates full of records. The prize possession of the house was a Hi-Fi record-player with a big enclosed speaker. It occupied the table directly across from the door.

They heard the toilet flush, and a moment later George Bavonette came out of the bedroom. He was handsome in a world-weary way, with long lashes, drooping lids, a waxy skin, large dark eyes. His mouth was tight and straight; he talked in staccato bursts, and never seemed to stop smoking. He never looked at Julie, Cathy, or Dean while speaking to them. They sat around the kitchen table drinking coffee, the girls making small-talk.

Presently George jumped to his feet, went into the living room, loaded records on the turntable, came back into the kitchen. The music started and George drummed his fingers on the table, leaned his chair back against the wall, smiling faintly to himself. Julie and Cathy exchanged glances.

"George throws so much of himself into his music he's got to get it back somehow," said Dean.

"Right, right," said George. "Expressed very well..."

Encouraged, Dean went on: "It's really a nerve-racking job — sitting at that piano night after night — creating, creating..."

"Takes lots of force," said George.

"It's bop — isn't it?" Julie asked brightly.

"No no!" cried George. "All bop is progressive. But all progressive isn't bop... Listen — now!" He held up his hand. "Get this idea — *now*!"

The piano tinkled oddly up the scale, paused, came hesitantly back down. In the center of a progression it stopped short; a tenor sax took over, blowing in a new discordant key.

George looked at them all. "Ain't that mad now?"

"I guess I'm stupid," said Julie. "It sounds queer and jangly..."

"My dear girl," said George, "how do you regard our present civilization? Isn't it queer and jangly too? That's why music is great; it's contemporary; it gets with the mood of our times."

"I don't think so," said Julie.

"It's kinda deep," said Dean. "George explains it very well. Go ahead, George."

"No. Not right now. I feel more like riding a fast horse."

"Joke," said Dean. "He can talk sense when he wants to."

"I'm interested," said Julie.

"You gotta feel it." George tapped his forehead. "It's gotta go on in here. Ideas. Sometimes it's wonderful; sometimes it's so much it scares you." He rose to his feet. "You kids like some breakfast? I'm shriveled."

"Heavens, no," said Cathy. "It's two o'clock."

"Two?" George glanced at the kitchen clock. "I want to be at Cholo's today..." He turned to Dean. "Look hon, knock me up a couple eggs while I get dressed."

Dean lit the old gas stove, put on a pan, scraped in some butter, broke a pair of eggs.

"George gets awful excited," said Dean in a confidential manner. "Don't think he's a smart aleck; he's not. He's just a little hipped on his music. He's awfully good, really; but oh my, is he unpredictable!" She looked fondly toward the bedroom. "Never a dull moment around here; I guess that's why I'm so crazy about him." She spoke a trifle too emphatically.

George came back in, ate swiftly, his head lowered. He looked in some surprise at Dean. "Get dressed. You're coming with me."

Dean hesitated, then smiled at Julie and Cathy. "We can all go, can't we George?" She said to Julie and Cathy, "It's a jam session — the boys just sit around and drink beer and play. It's really fun..."

George frowned. "It's rehearsal. Stolid, dull, uninteresting." He said to Julie and Cathy, "Don't expect any feats of skill."

"Please come," Dean said. "Please."

"Well," said Cathy, "I guess we could stay a little while."

Cholo lived on the top of Telegraph Hill. His apartment consisted of a single room forty feet long, with kitchen equipment at one end, studio couches at the other. The walls were pasted with light green burlap, reed mats covered the floor. Two old upright pianos stood along one wall; between them was a drum setup.

When George, Dean, Cathy and Julie arrived the room was empty.

"What the devil," said George. He yelled, "Hey, Cholo!" There was no response. He strode the length of the room, opened a door, stuck his head through; then turned, came back shaking his head.

"Oh, well," said George. He opened the icebox, looked inside. "The son of a gun shorted us. There's only three beers."

He opened the three cans, found four glasses, divided the beer. Dean served. George went over to the piano, ran his fingers over the scale. He turned with a look of sheer pleasure, "Why hon — old Cholo's fumigated the thing! Grease job, tune-up. Listen!" He struck out a scale. "Last week a man couldn't tell high C from a cowbell."

The door opened. Six men and four women streamed in. There were greetings, introductions, names which neither Julie nor Cathy remembered.

Cholo was a dapper young Italian, short, thin, full of merriment; he filled a pitcher with ice cubes, poured in a fifth of vodka, a pint of lime juice, set the pitcher on the piano. Two of the men unpacked tenor saxes; a middle-aged man with red hair brought out a trumpet. Cholo played electric guitar.

George sat down at the piano.

Julie and Cathy took seats at the far end of the room. Dean brought over three glasses of the vodka-lime juice, and sat down beside them. "Isn't this fun? It kinda gets in your blood, this way of life. It's free and easy... Of course half the time we don't know where our next meal's coming from. George is just crazy with money." She sighed, leaned back. "Have you seen anything of my folks?"

"Just Carr," said Cathy.

"Oh, Carr," said Dean. "He's the phoniest of the lot." Her voice was bitter. "He's not good enough to lick George's boots."

The music began. Up the scale, down the scale; across, back; tonal, atonal; sharp, flat; chords, discords.

A number of other people came in. Two young men came over to Julie and Cathy. They spoke of a party scheduled for next Friday night and invited the girls to it.

"I can't," said Julie. "I only get one night out a week. And I already have a date."

"Oh, you college chicks," said the one boy. "Well, let's work up a big time for week after next..."

"You chicks ever try the Green Bottle?" asked the other boy.

"No," said Cathy.

"That's a hangout for the crowd — maybe we could meet you there."

"We're too busy," said Julie. "Much too busy."

Dean was circulating at the far end of the room. She stopped in front of a young man in a tan tweed jacket sitting with his back to Cathy and Julie. They could look directly into Dean's face.

Cathy nudged Julie. "Marriage hasn't changed Dean very much."

"Hm," said Julie. "Definitely."

"Something tells me," said Cathy, "that our friend George doesn't like the guy."

Dean, laughing, took the young man's hands, leaned back.

The piano gave three harsh jangles. Everyone stopped playing. George rose to his feet and said in a loud voice, "Keep your hands off my wife!"

The young man turned his head. He looked surprised. "Sure."

Dean whirled away from him, cheeks flaming, and came to sit beside Cathy and Julie. The music began again.

"Damn that George!" muttered Dean. "I can't even talk to a man!"

Julie and Cathy said nothing.

Dean went on viciously, "He sure steps out whenever the mood takes him."

The young man in the tan jacket rose, waved to Cholo and left. George watched him go.

Cathy said, "I think it's about time we were going too."

"Oh, dear," said Dean. "There's so much I want to talk over..." She looked suddenly wistful and lonesome.

"Why don't you come over to the house someday?" said Cathy. "For lunch."

"George hardly lets me out of his sight," said Dean. She contemplated the back of her husband. "Oh well..." She forced a smile.

Cathy and Julie waved goodbye to George and left.

CHAPTER VI

IN EARLY MARCH Carr Pendry returned from Europe with a new Jaguar. He spent two days in San Giorgio then drove south to Berkeley. He drove up University Avenue, swung around the campus, and finally drew to a proud halt in front of the Delta Rho Beta house.

As luck would have it, Cathy herself answered the door.

"Cathy!"

"Why, Carr!" said Cathy.

"Well, I'm back," said Carr. "Look what I brought with me!" And he pointed to the Jag.

"How nice," said Cathy. "An MG, isn't it?"

"MG!" exclaimed Carr. "That's a Jaguar Mark IV, the undisputed lord of the road! Now get into your prettiest gown — we're going out!"

"Oh, Carr," said Cathy. "I've already got a date."

"You'll have to break it," announced Carr. "I haven't come six thousand miles just to be stopped by another date."

"Oh well," said Cathy. "I'll see what I can do... Come in."

Carr waited in the hall while Cathy ran upstairs to where Julie lay on her bed with a French grammar, memorizing vocabulary.

"Ouvrez la porte," said Julie. *"Avez-vous du pain..."*

"Julie — guess who's downstairs wearing a blue Jaguar."

"I give up."

"It's Carr."

"Sacre blue! *Nom d'un chien!"*

"He wants me to go out. I dread it. He'll be maudlin and messy."

"Tell him you have a date."

"I do and I did. He says to break it."

"Tell him you can't."

"Oh, Julie — that's bearing down pretty hard."

"Okay," shrugged Julie. "Go out with him."

"I want you to come along."

"Me? A third wheel? Carr would love that."

"You don't have a date?"

"Not with three midterms Monday. Think of it. Three on one day."

"Oh Julie. Come on. Don't be a grind. You can study all day tomorrow and Sunday."

"I don't have a date." Julie tossed away her book. "But I sure can get one in a hurry." She led Cathy to the upstairs telephone, thumbed through the Officers and Students Directory, called a number.

"Hello," said Julie. "May I speak to Joe Treddick please?"

Cathy asked in a hushed voice, "Who's Joe Treddick?"

"Man next to me in English... I think that's his name. I read it off one of his books." She turned back to the phone. "Hello? Is this Joe Treddick?... This is Julie Hovard. I sit next to you in English 1B... Well, I don't have a date and I'm wondering if you're doing anything... Oh rats. I've got three on Monday myself. I wouldn't go either, except it's a very special occasion... We'll go Dutch. I insist... Okay, thanks a lot. Eight o'clock." Julie hung up. "There. That was easy."

"You're shameless," said Cathy. "You even thank him."

"Sure. He's doing me a favor."

"Ha ha," laughed Cathy. "I'll bet he's just been afraid to ask you for a date."

"Not Joe," said Julie.

Carr was not pleased. "Cathy, can't we go somewhere by ourselves — wine by candlelight — look at each other —"

"Now, Carr, I've made myself hated once this evening; I can't do it again. Besides, we've got to be in early."

Carr turned away sulkily.

"I've got to dress," said Cathy. "You sit quiet, or go out and polish your Jaguar."

At eight o'clock the front doorbell rang. A freshman ran to the door. A muscular young man with dark hair and a heavily tanned skin stood outside.

"Will you tell Julie Hovard that Joe Treddick's here?"

"Right. Won't you come in?"

Joe Treddick had a quiet manner, and a face that was rugged and hard. He looked at Carr, nodded, sat down.

Julie appeared wearing a simple gray jersey dress, an infinitesimal white knit skullcap, and looking like a princess. She waved at Carr, grinned at Joe Treddick.

"Hello Joe."

"Hello, Julie."

She pitched her voice low, "If anyone asks, we've had this date for two or three days."

"Anything you like."

She glanced at Carr, who was watching her suspiciously. Then Cathy came into the room and Carr's attention was distracted.

"Carr is an old friend," said Julie hurriedly. "He's crazy about Cathy but she doesn't want to encourage him; so she asked me to go out with them."

Joe Treddick nodded. "I see."

Julie took his hand, led him to where Carr stood holding Cathy by her shoulders, devouring her with his eyes.

Cathy stood before him in pale beige, her dark hair long and lustrous, her eyes like melted amber, her mouth faintly tinted, tender as butter. She could have done nothing to make herself more beautiful. She had done her best to twist the knife in Carr's heart.

Carr suggested dinner-dancing at the Fairmont, but Cathy said in horror, "The prices, Carr!"

"Yes," said Julie. "Joe isn't a millionaire. We've got to be practical Carr."

"Who wants to be practical?" declared Carr loftily.

"Nobody wants to be," said Joe.

Carr gave in with the best grace he could muster. Since the four couldn't squeeze into the Jaguar, Julie drove her convertible, with Carr and Cathy in the back seat.

They drove across the bridge to San Francisco, and wandered from bar to bar: Green Dragon in Chinatown to the Paper Doll in North Beach to the Finnish Bar on the waterfront to the Club Hangover on

Bush Street. Carr took great pains with his conversation, formulating epigrams, sophisticated criticisms, clever wisecracks which somehow always belittled something or someone. And Carr made sure the conversation centered on San Giorgio and old times, with the effect of isolating Joe from the group.

Whatever Joe Treddick thought, he gave no outward sign. He listened politely, laughed at Carr's jokes and made no effort to compete. After a few drinks, Carr adopted a patronizing attitude.

"What are you studying, Joe?"

"I'm a civil engineer," said Joe.

"Sounds like a lot of hard work," said Carr with a laugh. "Myself, if I can make my brains do the work of my back, I'm all for it."

"It's no bed of roses," Joe admitted. "But if I wanted to scrounge my way through life, I'd go into something like politics."

Julie said brightly, "Carr is planning to run for state senator." And they all turned looks of speculation upon Carr.

"Have you been to see Dean?" Cathy asked Carr.

"No," said Carr shortly.

"We went to see her last winter, and she came over — oh, a couple weeks ago."

"How's she making out?"

"Well," said Cathy slowly, "she's not very happy... It must be like living with a — a leopard, living with George."

"What's wrong with him?"

"Oh — he's moody. And temperamental."

Carr sighed. "I guess I'll have to run over to see her... I bought her some French perfume; got it in Grasse. Only suckers buy it in Paris. Get a jugful of any blend you can name if you know where to look for it. Naturally you've got to have a nose; otherwise they'll palm off after-shave lotion on you. Same way with wines. They think that just because you're an American you have no taste." He sat back, pleased with himself. "If you ever plan to go to Europe, Joe," he said in a fatherly voice, "let me know and I'll give you a few pointers."

"Thanks," said Joe. "But I won't be going back for a while."

"Oh," said Carr. "You've been there."

"Off and on."

"Off and on? I don't get you."

"I'm an ex-seaman."

"Oh, Navy."

"No. Merchant-seaman. I've got third-mate papers. Panamanian third-mate papers I should say. Anybody that can read can get 'em."

"That sounds like fun!" said Julie.

"You don't see much perfume or vintage wine. You drink with the rest of the peasants. *Vino rosso* — schnapps — *slivowitz* — *retzina*... In the Pacific there's always betel nut."

"Oh," cried Julie in excitement. "That's the way I'd like to travel. Anybody can buy their way."

Carr sat looking stonily into his highball. He thought never in his life had he disliked anyone as much as Joe Treddick.

At one o'clock Cathy insisted on going home.

Back at the house Carr wanted Cathy to go for a ride in the Jag, but Cathy said she had to sign in.

Joe got out on the sidewalk to walk Julie up to the door, but she said, "Jump in Joe. I'll drive you home."

Joe got in and Julie started the car. "You tell me where."

"Barrington Hall."

She said, "I hope you weren't too bored... Carr is rather a pill. We've known him all our lives. That makes him different, I guess."

"I had a good time," said Joe.

"I said we'd go Dutch," Julie laughed. "But I don't know how to go about giving you money."

Joe smiled. "Forget it."

She stopped in front of Joe's rooming house. Joe got out.

"Good night, Julie."

"Good night Joe."

"Joe?"

"Yes?"

"Do you think I'm a spoiled brat, a typical sorority snob with too much money and a superiority complex?"

"I hadn't thought about it too much."

"But if you thought so, you wouldn't want to go out with me again."

"No," said Joe smiling faintly. "I guess I wouldn't."

"Well," said Julie, "I can't go anyway until after midterms — so you can ask me then."

"Okay," said Joe. "Good night."

"Good night, Joe."

Joe watched the red taillights dwindle up the street.

Carr Pendry decided to put it off no longer. After all, she was his sister.

He thought over the visit very carefully. He did not want to meet the husband, this piano-playing fellow — it would somehow set the seal of family approval on him.

He drove the Jaguar to San Francisco, looked up the address of the Kalmyra Club, and drove there. The Kalmyra Club was a luxurious place, and Carr was surprised. He had expected something ratty.

He made his way to the bar on a mezzanine, ordered a Scotch and soda, and made a careful inspection of the place.

It was intermission; the musicians were off the stand. A short colored man idled up on the dais, picked up his tenor sax and began blowing. Carr, for the life of him, couldn't follow the tune. It was soft and quiet; still, it seemed utterly disjointed and discordant. A moment later the piano player and the steel-guitar man joined him on the dais, and the Manley Hatch Trio was in session.

Carr ignored the music and studied the piano-player. So this was George Bavonette. His brother-in-law. He looked distinguished, stern, intent on his music. His skin was pale, his eyes bright.

George took an extended solo, finished, accepted applause with a curt nod. "Boy," said a man beside Carr, "tonight he's great."

Carr went to the telephone and called the number Cathy had given him.

Dean answered.

"Hello Dean. This is Carr."

"Carr?" Dean's voice was tremulous and harsh at once.

"Yes. Carr. I'll be at your apartment in ten minutes."

Dean's voice was clouded. "Okay Carr."

The apartment was closer than he had expected; he made it in five minutes. He found the name on the directory: *George and Dean Bavonette, Apt. 32.* He pressed the bell smartly, noticed the door was not quite closed, and walked in. There was no elevator; Carr climbed the carpeted stairs to the third floor.

He stopped at the head of the stairs, cursing the management for providing such inadequate lights.

To the left, at the far end of the corridor, stood a man in a tan jacket and gray flannels. The man was looking out the window marked FIRE ESCAPE, with his back to Carr.

Carr turned down the corridor to the right, and found 32. He rapped; the door opened; Dean stood back. "Come in, Carr."

Carr slowly stepped into the apartment, turned back to look at Dean. He was shocked.

She wore lounging pajamas and a bathrobe. Her face was flushed and dazed, her lipstick was blotched and her hair was tangled. She looked thirty years old.

"Sit down Carr. Sit down," she said in a breathless voice.

"What's the matter?" Carr demanded sharply. "You're acting queer."

"Ha." She laughed — a soft-breathed laugh of wonder. "Ha... You'd be acting queer, too."

Carr handed her a small package. "I brought you this from France."

Dean took the package and put it on the table. Carr watched in irritation. Dean came to some kind of decision.

"Carr."

"Well?"

"Something just happened. You'd never guess what."

"No," snapped Carr. "I suppose I wouldn't."

Dean leaned back against the record shelves. "You just missed an old friend."

"Are you drunk? Or doped?"

She smiled. "I wish I were. I feel funny, as if I'd seen a ghost."

"Oh, cut the dramatics."

Dean ran her hand through her shaggy auburn hair, sat down beside him. "Carr — do you remember Robert Struve?"

Carr blinked, shifted mental gears. "Naturally. What about him?"

"You missed him by about a minute."

"I'll be damned!" He looked at her with narrowed eyes. "Was he wearing a tan coat?"

"Something like that. A tan tweed jacket."

"Mmph," muttered Carr. "I saw him in the hall. He had his back to me. By golly, I thought he looked vaguely familiar!" He glanced sharply at Dean. "What was he doing here?"

"Oh — well —" Her voice faltered.

"But great Gadfrey! Robert Struve! How could you stand it?"

"He's changed. Oh, how he's changed..."

Carr shook his head like an angry bull. "I don't get it — don't get it at all. What's he doing here in the first place?"

Dean looked moodily at her feet. "Oh — well, if the truth were known — and I guess it is — I don't get along too well with George," she said angrily. "He treats me like a — a card table. Something you can pull out and use when you need it, then fold up and push back out of the way. Well," her voice became hesitant again, "I met — Robert. He knew me, but I didn't know him. He's going under a different name."

"Go on," he said in a clipped voice.

"I met him. I liked him. There was something about him..." She contemplated the image in her mind. "Well, George suspected the worst right away; he nagged something awful. So I kept seeing — Robert."

"Go on," he said.

"There's not much to say, really. It's just the weird way this whole thing worked out. Here's this fellow you think is a nice guy, a stranger. You get to like him; you act a little foolish and then suddenly you look at him, and you see he's really someone else in disguise. Someone kinda horrible."

"What's wrong with him?" asked Carr curiously.

She shook her head in perplexity. "He always was a peculiar kind of guy. Remember how he was in football? He'd go a little crazy. He'd get the ball, and they could break his legs but they couldn't stop him."

"What's that got to do with you? You never did anything to him."

"I asked him that," said Dean. "I said, 'We were always friendly, Robert. How come you look at me like that?'

" 'Dean,' he said, 'a salmon is born; it floats down the river into the ocean. Then years later it comes back. It's got a mission. It doesn't have any choice. It's driven by its inner necessity.'

" 'Yeah,' I told him, 'but you're not a salmon.'

" 'No — but I have compulsions. I know enough to realize what they are, and the only way I'll get rid of them.' "

Carr asked, "What kind of compulsions? Did he say?"

Dean shook her head. "I didn't pretend to understand him, and where he got all that psychological lore I don't know."

"Let's see," said Carr. "He's been out of jail — oh, over a year now, I guess. I suppose he's bitter."

"He got a bum deal. But it wasn't my fault."

"Maybe he got what he was after," suggested Carr. "Maybe you're imagining all the other."

"Imagining!" cried Dean. "I don't know what I'm imagining... I don't know what he's thinking! I'm scared —"

"Scared? What's there to be scared of?"

Dean said miserably, "I don't know."

Carr rose to his feet. "Well — if I were you, I'd go home to San Giorgio. Mother's mad, but not so you couldn't bring her around. Actually she'd be glad to see you."

"I feel sorry for George," said Dean. "He's really a nice guy once you get inside him... I wouldn't want to hurt him."

Carr put his hand on the doorknob. "I'll be going... Anything you want me to tell Mother?"

Dean looked out the window. "I'll give her a ring one of these days. Maybe tomorrow. When I figure things out just a little."

"Goodbye," said Carr. He left.

Dean sat back down on the sofa, her legs stretched ungracefully out in front of her. She saw Carr's present, but lacked the energy to open it. She thought about coffee, rejected the idea. She thought about Robert Struve...

The door opened. Dean saw who it was, looked at him in surprise. "Hello," she said in a husky voice. "This is — unexpected."

"I thought it would be." He came over beside her. She saw that he carried a butcher knife. Her voice clogged in her throat. "What — what are you doing?"

"I've decided to kill you."

"No — you can't. You've had what you wanted from me," she croaked. "I've given you everything you wanted."

He shook his head. "No. No. No." He put his left hand in her hair; she stared up at him limply. He stabbed her in the throat. After a moment he bent forward, slashed at her face, hacking, slicing. Panting, he stood back.

He went to the bathroom, took off his rubber gloves, washed his hands. From the kitchen he brought a paper sack, stuffed in the gloves and the knife.

At the door he looked back to the couch and the sprawled horrid mess. He compressed his mouth, shook his head slightly, and left.

Chapter VII

Carr went to a telephone, called the Delta Rho Beta house. "Cathy McDermott, please."

"Sorry, she's out for the evening. Would you care to leave your name?" a voice said.

"Tell her Carr Pendry called."

Carr returned to the bar and finished his highball. He was jealous, lonesome, uneasy, unhappy. Things weren't going right. It was hard to be angry with Cathy; but after all, she was his girl; that's the way it had been for years.

Images began to flow into Carr's mind, pictures of Cathy dancing with some other man, parking with him, kissing him... He gulped down his drink. He'd show her. Two could play that game. He signaled the bartender.

"Yes sir?"

"Say," said Carr, "where can a man find a little high-class entertainment?"

The bartender looked off into space. "Sure I don't know, mister." He went away, and came back with a card. "I found this on the floor the other day. Personally I don't know nothing about it."

"Thanks," said Carr.

"Yes sir," said the bartender.

The evening was still young when Carr returned to the street. The Kalmyra Club was not far distant; he wandered in. Manley Hatch's Trio was in full cry.

George took a long solo, his austere profile intent over the keys. His fingers made fantastic sounds, a bewildering succession of non-melodic phrases.

He finished to a storm of applause. Carr looked around in frowning puzzlement. What was in this music? Was there something he didn't understand?

His second highball conveyed only the faintest flavor of whisky to his palate. He called the barmaid back. "Take away this slop and bring me a drink."

"Yes, sir."

She brought him another, very little better. Perhaps it was the same drink. Fuming, he let it stand on the table.

The set ended; George Bavonette sauntered past. Carr reached out and caught his coat. George looked down with a frown. "If you want a souvenir, I'll give you my autograph."

"Sit down," said Carr. "I want to talk to you."

"Can't be done," said George, and started to walk away.

"About Dean," said Carr.

George whirled. "What about her?"

"I'm her brother," said Carr.

George looked down at him with glowing eyes. "You're her brother, are you? Her royal brother. What are you doing here?"

"Just looked in," said Carr. "That music is very interesting."

George settled himself into a chair. "How come this swift brotherly love?"

"I just got back from Europe," said Carr. "This is the first chance I've had to see Dean."

"Oh," said George, "you saw Dean, did you?"

"Yes. Early this evening."

George nodded. "How many guys ran out the back when you opened the door?"

Carr said frigidly, "There's no call for that kind of talk."

"Ha!" laughed George. "It makes no difference now. Because the song is ended. From now on —" he made a flat gesture "— she digs her jive; I dig mine."

"You mean," said Carr in sudden hope, "that you're planning to leave her?"

George rose to his feet. "Leave her? Man, I done left. I'm gone." He made a casual sign of farewell and sauntered away.

Carr sat thinking. This was good news. Dean could come back with him to San Giorgio, plan a new life for herself.

Carr left the Kalmyra and drove to the apartment. As before, the door was ajar. He ascended the steps, knocked at the door to 32.

No answer.

He tried the door. It swung open.

About three o'clock the police let Carr go. He drove in a dream to the Fairmont, booked a room, rode glassy-eyed up in the elevator. He staggered into his room, slipped down in a chair and broke into a dry sobbing.

The face so familiar, now so dreadfully strange, with all the secrets of its structure laid open… He clenched and unclenched his fists. When they caught the murderer —

When they caught the murderer. Would they catch him? So many of these crimes were unsolved —

By God, he'd see they solved this one! He'd keep riding them until they pulled someone in! Lieutenant Spargill of Homicide seemed efficient enough — a tall sensitive-looking man with thin sandy hair.

Carr had told him everything: about Dean's unhappy marriage, her peculiar affair with Robert Struve. "Just tonight she told me she was afraid of him. He threatened her."

"Robert Struve, eh? Where's he live?"

"Well, I don't know."

"What's he look like?"

"I'm afraid I don't know that either. And it's probably not the name he's going under."

"You don't know the name he's using?"

"She never mentioned it. I meant to ask and forgot." Carr jumped up from his chair, strode back and forth. "If only I could lay my hands on the fellow…"

"Just relax, Mr. Pendry. We'll get him…"

Up in his hotel room Carr presently fell asleep.

He woke up with a fearful headache. He called Room Service and ordered coffee, then forced himself to telephone San Giorgio.

The conversation was as bad as he had feared. Worse. He prevailed upon his father not to come down to San Francisco, and promised to return to San Giorgio at once.

At ten o'clock he called Lieutenant Spargill. Spargill was polite but evasive.

"We're looking the situation over, Mr. Pendry. In fact, I think we're getting to the bottom of it."

"Good!" said Carr savagely. "I hope you hang him higher than a kite."

"We'll certainly do our best."

"Is there any reason why I should stay in San Francisco?"

"Why no, I guess not. Where will you be if we need you?"

"In San Giorgio. You have my home address."

"Very well, Mr. Pendry. We'll call you if we need you."

When Carr arrived in San Giorgio the *Herald-Republican* had already headlined the news:

LOCAL GIRL FALLS VICTIM TO MUTILATION MURDERER

Carr's mother was in bed under sedatives; his father was dangerously taut. Carr told the whole story again. "You probably don't remember him. He never ran with our crowd."

"Struve," said Pendry, a thin man with silky gray-blond hair and a dapper mustache. "Robert Struve. I can't place him."

"He's the kid that wrecked my motor-scooter, remember?"

"Oh, yes..."

The *Herald-Republican* got news of the arrest before the Pendrys. Carr read the story with amazement. "They've taken her husband. They've arrested Bavonette!"

"Bavonette!" said his father. "But you said..."

"There's been a terrible mistake," Carr muttered. "I talked to George myself down at the night club."

Pelton Pendry frowned dubiously. "They wouldn't move unless they were pretty certain."

"I know those cops," said Carr viciously. "They grab whoever looks easiest and call it a case. They probably just don't know where to find Struve." Carr rose to his feet. "I'm going down there."

"Maybe I'd better come, too," said Pelton Pendry.

*

Lieutenant Spargill greeted them with courtesy. "There's no question about it," he told them. "Bavonette did the killing."

"But I saw him myself!" cried Carr. "I talked to him in the Kalmyra Club."

"Yes, but how long after you'd left your sister?"

"Oh—" Carr blinked and fell suddenly quiet.

"Well?"

"I guess it was a couple hours," said Carr. "Around eleven-thirty."

Spargill nodded. "There you are."

"But surely—when he's playing in a night club he can't get away without someone noticing!"

"From nine forty-five till almost ten minutes after ten, the band took an intermission. He had all the time he needed."

"That still doesn't prove anything. Dean was afraid of this Robert Struve! He'd threatened her! He was—"

Lieutenant Spargill interrupted: "George Bavonette was known to be insanely jealous. Dean was known—well—begging your pardon—well, she was a pretty friendly girl. On more than one occasion they quarreled."

"Yes, but—"

"Then, there's evidence which we haven't released to the papers. In strict confidence—we've found the murder weapon and a pair of rubber gloves. They were in a paper bag in the garbage pail behind the Kalmyra Club."

"Couldn't it be a plant?" asked Carr in a subdued voice.

"We'll check every angle," said Spargill. "But I'm sure we've got our man. These things fall into a pattern."

A quiet funeral was held the next day, and Dean Pendry was laid to rest in the family plot.

There was a follow-up on the murder story in the *Herald-Republican.* George Bavonette had confessed to the killing.

Carr Pendry hurled the paper to the floor. "This thing is a frame-up!"

"He admits it, doesn't he?" his mother inquired. "He wouldn't say he did it if he hadn't done it." Her eyes were inflamed, but after five days she was able to speak without lapsing into tears.

"You don't know these cops," said Carr. "Bavonette is unstable. He'd confess anything if they kept after him long enough. I'm going down and talk to the guy myself."

He had no difficulty about seeing Bavonette, who came up to the netting with a face like a gaunt marble mask.

"Hello," said Carr, trying to keep his voice from shaking. After all, this *might* be the guilty man. "You remember me?" he asked. "I'm Dean's brother."

"Yeah," said George. "I place you now."

Carr delivered the speech he had rehearsed. "I read in the newspaper that you had confessed."

George sat looking at Carr.

Carr said, "But we're not convinced you're the guilty man."

George said nothing.

"Well," Carr asked sharply, "did you do it?"

"So they say."

"Did they force a confession out of you?"

"I didn't sing out of joy."

"Do you have a lawyer?"

"What good's a lawyer? They got me cold."

Carr nodded. "You don't want to give up hope. Plead not guilty. Say they forced the confession out of you. I know who really did the killing."

George showed a flicker of interest. "You do, do you? What are you going to do about it?"

"All I can. But I'd like some help from you."

"I can't give you any help. They got me here in the clink. You can see that for yourself."

"I mean information."

"I don't know *nothing*."

Carr assured him his interests would be safeguarded, and departed. He telephoned Cathy, then drove to the Delta Rho Beta house.

"Let's go out where we can talk," he suggested.

"We can talk here," said Cathy. "I've got two books to read before tomorrow."

Carr said testily, "Sometimes I'd like to find you without twenty other things to do."

"Oh, calm down Carr," said Cathy soothingly. "It doesn't make any difference, really."

"Oh no?" She was wearing blue jeans and a yellow sweater. He ran his eyes up her body, and she moved uncomfortably.

"Oh, stop it Carr." She settled into the corner of a couch, one leg under her. "We all feel terrible about Dean."

Carr nodded with a kind of determined belligerence. "Whoever did it — he's not going to get away with it."

Cathy was surprised. " 'Whoever' did it? George did it!"

Carr shrugged. "I'm not so sure. I just saw him."

"What did he say? Does he say he didn't do it?"

"Well, not in so many words. But I saw Dean, you know — I guess it wasn't an hour before she was killed."

Julie came into the room. "Hello Carr."

Cathy made room for her on the couch. "We're talking about Dean."

"Oh." Julie sat down. "What's new?"

"I'm not so sure that George did it," said Carr.

"Why?"

"Dean told me something, only about an hour before she — before it happened. Did you know that she was having a love affair?"

Julie shrugged. "Dean was always in love with four different men."

"Well, you'd never guess who her boy friend was."

"Who?"

"Robert Struve."

"You mean — *our* Robert Struve? From San Giorgio?"

"That's right."

"But —"

"She didn't recognize him — his face was fixed. Plastic surgery, I suppose. And he was going by a different name. She told me that he threatened her, said he had a compulsion."

"Compulsion to do what?"

"To do what he did do, I suppose."

Cathy said, "Did you tell the police?"

"Sure I told the police. Then they picked up George, and bulldozed him into a confession."

"And now he says he didn't do it?"

"He doesn't say much of anything."

Julie said dubiously, "They must be pretty sure, Carr. They wouldn't arrest George unless they know."

"My dear young woman," said Carr loftily, "cops are *people*!"

"That's what I mean," said Julie.

"All that aside," said Carr. "Just on the chance I'm right, and Struve is a madman — just watch your step."

Julie said, "He wouldn't have any reason to bother us."

"He didn't have any reason to bother Dean. And all he did was slice up her face till there wasn't any left!"

Chapter VIII

George Bavonette was tried for the murder of Dean Pendry Bavonette, and the issue was never in doubt. He pleaded not guilty by reason of insanity, but the jury barely left the box before returning with the verdict: guilty as charged.

The judge sentenced George Bavonette to death in the gas chamber, and Bavonette listened with a drooping mouth, his fingers drumming an eccentric rhythm on the oak rail.

Carr Pendry had an angry interview with the lawyer. "That was no defense at all—'by reason of insanity'! You should have pleaded 'not guilty' and fought it right down the line!"

The lawyer shook his head with cool courtesy. "There wasn't a chance, Mr. Pendry. You're not reckoning with the weight of the evidence against Bavonette. The best we could hope for was insanity. It was clearly the work of an unbalanced mind."

"I agree," snapped Carr. "But why not pin it on the real murderer?"

"How can you be so sure Bavonette is innocent? There's not a whit of evidence that he didn't do it."

"I'm going by what my sister told me."

"That's proof of nothing."

Two weeks earlier, Joe Treddick had told Julie that next Saturday he was driving down to Monterey, and asked if she'd like to come.

"Sure," said Julie. "So long as I get back by six or seven. It's the Interfraternity Ball and I've got a date. What's going on in Monterey?"

"I've got to get a job for the summer. A friend of mine—an old shipmate—has a fishing boat. I might as well catch fish as anything else."

They were drinking coffee in Jack's Restaurant outside of Sather Gate. Julie, looking out the window, raised her hand to a tall dark-haired young man with an arrogant high-bridged nose, deep-set black eyes, walking south on Telegraph.

"That's Tex Hanna," said Julie. "Kappa Alpha. My date for the Inter-fraternity Ball." She watched Joe like a kitten gauging the reaction of a cricket it had just patted.

Joe looked after Tex Hanna, then back at Julie. "Nice-looking fellow."

Julie drank her coffee. Joe's reactions were never predictable, though he was probably no older than Tex; certainly not as old as Carr.

Joe relaxed, watching her with an air of quiet appraisal that made Julie feel pleasantly self-conscious.

At eight o'clock Saturday morning Joe parked his weathered blue Plymouth sedan in front of the Delta Rho Beta house and Julie came running down the walk. She was wearing a dark blue pull-over, a faded-blue denim skirt.

"You're prompt," Julie told him as she got into the car.

"So are you."

"Oh, I've got all kinds of virtues."

They drove south with the sun phosphorescing through a high mist that swirled in across the bay from San Francisco. At San Jose the mist was gone and the sun was yellow. At Monterey a wind blew in off the Pacific from the direction of Hawaii, twisting the black cypress, flecking the face of the ocean with whitecaps.

Joe parked in front of Fisherman's Wharf; they got out, walked down the pier. Below them the white and blue fishing boats heaved and moaned at the moorings. The air smelt of tar and fish; infinitesimal drops of salt water blew in their faces. Joe stopped halfway down the pier, frowned at a small dirty gray trawler. He pulled a letter from his pocket, checked the number of the berth.

"This is the right place, but the wrong boat," said Joe.

A curly-haired Italian came up out of the gray trawler with a bucket of bilge water.

"Hey," Joe called down. "Where's the *Consuela*?"

"She's gone. Two weeks ago. I think San Diego."

"Thanks."

Joe and Julie walked back down the pier. Julie took his arm.

"That's too bad, Joe."

"It was just an off chance." He looked at his watch. "Eleven-thirty. How about some lunch?"

"I'm hungry."

They had clam chowder and fried fish in a restaurant at the head of the wharf. Joe seemed restless and tense. Julie was puzzled. It hardly seemed likely that missing the fishing boat would upset him.

After lunch they walked down along the waterfront, the sea gulls wheeling and crying overhead, the wind blowing in their faces, and stood looking out across the ocean.

Joe picked up a rock, tossed it out into the surf. He laughed. "I get restless around salt water."

"Oh," said Julie. "Is *that* why you're so moody!"

"I suppose so… Look." He pointed to a sailboat moored to a buoy. "A Tahiti ketch. We could go anywhere in the world in that."

" 'We'?" Julie tugged at his arm. "You haven't even proposed yet."

"Boats run into money. That ketch would come to five or six thousand dollars. Another thousand to fit it out. A couple thousand to live on…"

"We'll start saving," said Julie. "I spend all sorts of money on Cokes and lipstick."

"I could cut out eating," said Joe.

They started back to Berkeley, neither one saying much, and at four-thirty arrived at the Delta Rho Beta house. The afternoon was crisp and overcast; young men and women were hurrying along the street.

"I won't ask you in," said Julie. "The house'll be in an uproar."

"Have fun," said Joe.

Julie felt vaguely guilty. The Inter-fraternity Ball would be rich with glamour, glitter, smooth music. Julie wanted to ask Joe where he was going tonight, what he would be doing, but couldn't.

She squeezed his hand. "I had a lovely time, Joe, even though you didn't get a job."

"Who wants to work?" said Joe. "Well, so long."

"'Bye, Joe."

She watched him drive down the street, then turned and went in the house.

The Inter-fraternity Ball was a great success, and so was Julie. She wore a new formal of gray and white striped cotton. Tex Hanna brought her a cluster of white orchids which she wore in her hair. At one-thirty the orchestra played *Good Night Sweetheart*; the musicians packed their instruments; the lights dimmed; the young men in tuxedos eddied out into the lobby with the girls in formals.

Tex Hanna and Julie met Cathy and her date, Tom Shaw, at Foster's for coffee and doughnuts; then they drove back across the bridge for the two-thirty lockout.

Tex came up to the porch with Julie, kissed her good night.

Julie said, "I had a wonderful time Tex," which she had, and stepped inside.

She paused in the downstairs hall. She was excited, stimulated by the music and dancing and highballs, and by the idea that she'd had for the last two hours. She looked at the grandfather's clock. 2:12. Eighteen minutes to lockout. The idea just wouldn't keep. She opened the door. No one was in sight.

She ran down the walk to her car and drove to Barrington Hall. Here she paused uncertainly, looking up at the five-storied mass of concrete. She couldn't very well go to the door. If she knew Joe's window, she might be able to throw gravel. One or two lights were glowing. One of them might be Joe's.

A car pulled up behind her. The headlights flicked off, the motor died. A young man got out and started up the steps.

"Hi," Julie called.

He turned, came over to the convertible, picturing sudden wonderful impossible events. "Hi!"

Julie smelled beer on his breath. "Do me a favor," she said. "If Joe Treddick is up, would you tell him I want to see him?"

He peered waggishly in at Julie. "Won't I do?"

"Not tonight."

The young man turned sadly, went inside. Julie sat fidgeting, looking at her watch.

Joe came out, still dressed in gray slacks and dark sweater. He looked her over. "My, you look beautiful."

Julie was tremendously glad she had come. "I can only stay a minute. I had a wonderful idea — and I just couldn't wait to tell you."

He leaned forward, his arms on the door. "What kind of idea?"

"Next week — Saturday — I want you to come home with me, up to San Giorgio. We'll come back Sunday. Okay?"

Joe looked at her thoughtfully. "Okay. But why?"

"Summer job."

"For me?"

She nodded.

Joe straightened up a little. Julie reached out and took his hand. "Now Joe, don't be proud!"

"Me, proud?" said Joe. "I don't have any pride."

"Of course you do. I've been worrying about you all evening."

Joe grinned. "Your date must have loved it."

"Oh, he didn't know. I'd hardly discuss it with him."

"I imagine not...What kind of job?"

"There's at least three possibilities... But we'll talk about it later; I've got to rush back. Okay?"

"Okay."

"Good night, Joe."

"Good night."

Julie made a screeching U-turn, gunned the convertible back up the hill. She parked, ran up the walk, burst through the door with thirty seconds to spare. Cathy McDermott, on her way up the steps, looked over the bannister.

"Julie Hovard! I thought you were home ages ago."

Julie ran up the stairs. "I've got lots to tell you..."

Cathy was dubious about the whole idea; she vaguely disapproved of Joe. Her values were based on social acceptance, convention, good form. She tried to explain to Julie, and since she wasn't able to define her faint distrust, she invented reasons.

Julie scoffed at her.

Actually, Cathy could find nothing about Joe to criticize. His conduct was irreproachable. Julie revealed that he had never even tried to kiss her.

Cathy was surprised. "Why do you go out with him?"

"Oh, he'll get around to it sometime," said Julie. "Why don't you come home next weekend too?"

"I've got a date," said Cathy. "Tom Shaw."

"Bring him along."

"I suppose I could..."

Cathy finally agreed; and next Saturday the four drove north in Julie's convertible.

Thus, when Carr Pendry telephoned the Delta Rho Beta house after the conviction and sentencing of George Bavonette, he was notified that Cathy had gone home for the weekend.

He arrived in San Giorgio at three, parked the Jag, went to the McDermott house, where Mrs. McDermott told him that Cathy was swimming at the Hovards'. Carr marched out on the Hovard terrace to find Julie, Joe, Cathy and Tom Shaw lying beside the pool in the sun. Joe Treddick and Tom Shaw were elements he had not bargained for. Resentful and warm in his tweed suit, he dropped into a deck chair. "Well—they've convicted Bavonette. He goes to the gas chamber July seventh."

There was a silence. Presently Julie said, "Well, I guess he has it coming to him."

"Hah!" Carr snorted. He lit a cigarette, leaned back and blew smoke violently through his nose. "I still don't think he did it. That poor fool of a Bavonette's hypnotized himself."

"But surely, he'd never admit a murder!" Julie protested.

"My dear child," said Carr, "just read any good textbook of Freudian psychology. Read about guilt complexes, the will-to-death."

"But why, Carr? Why should he feel guilty?"

"I don't know," said Carr. "After all, we don't know a thing about Bavonette's past."

"Go get your bathing trunks, Carr," said Julie. "You look all warm and flustered."

Carr sized up Tom Shaw, gauging his own physique against Shaw's. Deciding that it would hold up reasonably well, he jumped to his feet, cut through the garden to the Pendry home.

"Poor Carr," said Julie. "Talk about complexes. He'll drive himself nuts trying to prove that Robert Struve killed Dean."

"Who's Robert Struve?" asked Tom Shaw.

"Oh, a poor unfortunate kid we used to know."

"Carr thinks he killed Dean," said Cathy. "I suppose it's not impossible."

"My first love," said Julie, with a sly glance at Cathy, who looked embarrassed. Alone of all Julie's friends, Cathy knew the whole truth of what had happened; like Julie's mother, she had been much more upset than Julie.

Julie had all but forgotten the incident. When she thought of Robert Struve two sharp images came to her mind. The first was a flash of blue shirt on a red motor-scooter, with Jamaica Arch ahead. Then the hateful thump, the muffled clatter of motor-scooter in the culvert... The second was the recollection of a football game during her freshman year at high school. The Paytonville team was big and tough. For three quarters the score had been tied at 6 to 6. In the last minutes of the fourth quarter San Giorgio took the ball deep in its own territory.

Bob Goble handed off to Robert Struve, who, after an almost deliberate start, began to churn forward. Three men brought him down after six yards.

Third down; Goble to Struve. Again the slow gathering of force, the almost insolent deliberateness. Another six yards.

Goble to Struve: the same play, with now the whole Paytonville team waiting. Struve might have avoided them, but lowered his head and plunged dead into the middle of them. Another six yards.

San Giorgio was yelling. "Six yards, Robert! Six yards!"

Seven yards. Six yards. Five yards.

This was Julie's second recollection of Robert Struve: under the wire frame, his face had been grotesque, magnificent, like an Aztec war mask.

At dinner, Darrell Hovard was full of talk about the new country club. Ground was being broken for construction, bulldozers were already shaping the golf course.

Julie came directly to the point. "Father, Joe's looking for a summer job. Why can't he work up at Mountainview?"

Joe's jaw dropped. He had expected nothing like this.

"Why, dear," said Darrell Hovard, "that's something quite out of my hands. All the work is contracted."

"I know; but if you were to speak to one of the contractors..."

Joe made an uncomfortable protest, but Julie ignored him.

"You could, couldn't you, Father?"

Darrell Hovard turned Joe a glance of careful speculation. "Just what are you able to do, Joe?"

"Really, Mr. Hovard, I didn't—"

Margaret interceded. "Julie, dear, don't insist! Perhaps Joe doesn't want to be stuck all summer in a dull place like San Giorgio."

"It isn't that, Mrs. Hovard—"

"Joe," said Julie, "tell Father what, if anything, you can do."

"I've got a strong back," said Joe.

"Oh, Joe," said Julie. "He's studying to be an engineer, Father."

After a telephone call it was arranged that Joe should go to work driving a dump truck immediately after finals.

Chapter IX

When Julie dropped Joe off in front of Barrington Hall late Sunday night, both knew their relationship had reached a critical stage. They had to go forward, or go back. If Joe had not risen to the occasion — well, Julie did not know what she would have done.

But Joe did not fail her. He put an arm around her, kissed her willing mouth, then the tip of her nose.

"The end of a perfect weekend," said Julie.

"It was nice," said Joe. After a minute he said, "Too nice."

"Nothing's really too nice," said Julie. "It never can be."

Joe looked down at her, and she felt he was about to say something important. But he was silent.

"Tell me what you're thinking."

Joe sighed. "Julie — you couldn't understand unless you've had something wonderful that got taken away from you ... I don't imagine you ever have."

"No." She squeezed his hand. "But I can imagine ..."

"Well — think of it in terms of goals ..."

Julie drew away, looked at him searchingly. "Just what are these goals — or should I ask?"

Joe laughed. "The first and most important is named Julie Hovard."

"Would you deceive me Joe?"

"No, Julie."

"You're sure? Absolutely, positively, definitely sure?"

"Yes."

"In that case —" She put her arms around his neck; and he held her tighter and longer and harder than she had ever let anyone hold her before.

Joe released her and got out of the car. She felt an undercurrent in him, and it puzzled her...Well, there was lots of time to find out. She waved, started the car and drove back to the Delta Rho Beta house.

Cathy surveyed her with raised eyebrows. "Your lipstick's smeared."

"Of course it is," said Julie. She suddenly felt like hugging Cathy, and did so.

"You're just gushing over with it, aren't you? Just like a little puppy-dog."

Julie yapped like a puppy and went chattering off to bed.

There were two weeks of final examinations, then freedom!

Julie had been home two days when Joe telephoned.

"Joe! Where are you?"

"In San Giorgio...I go to work in the morning."

"But where are you now? You're coming on out, aren't you?"

"I've got to find a place to stay and I need a working permit from the union."

"There's a place out on Second Street. The Fair Oaks Guest House. It's old-fashioned, but it's nice and quiet."

"I'll go there first thing."

Margaret Hovard came into the room as Julie hung up. She asked, "Who's that, dear?"

"It's Joe. He'll be out for dinner."

Margaret put on a faint frown of puzzlement. "'Joe'?"

"Joe Treddick."

Margaret pretended to search her mind. "You have so many young men. It's hard to keep abreast of them all."

Julie explained who Joe was.

"Oh," said Margaret. "That one." She and Darrell had not particularly approved of Joe. "Don't you think he's just a little — dull?"

"Dull?" exclaimed Julie in amusement. "I certainly don't."

"He never has much to say," said Margaret. "Norman Baker, for instance — he's so bright and amusing."

"He works himself sick for laughs."

"Well, Carr...I don't see why you don't take more of an interest in Carr."

Julie laughed in sheer enjoyment of her mother's naiveté. "Carr means well, but he's really so narrow-minded."

"I think he's very sound. And I don't understand what you see in Joe."

"There's such a lot to him."

Darrell Hovard came home and joined the conversation. He didn't object to Joe personally, but he liked to know a little more about the young men Julie went out with.

Margaret asked Julie if she had ever met any of Joe's people. "No," said Julie. "They're back in Boston."

"But who are they?"

Julie supposed they were ordinary mortals like anyone else. Darrell changed the subject; he did not want to make an issue of Joe. In a month or two Julie would be eighteen, when she could marry whomever she wanted. Darrell didn't want to put any romantic ideas into her head.

He had a quiet word with Margaret before dinner. "Give her time," said Darrell. "She's growing up. All girls have their little affairs before settling down; Julie's no different from the others."

"I'm not so sure."

"You'll see," said Darrell.

"I just don't like to leave things to chance," said Margaret.

Darrell thought the situation over. "Well—there's rather a mean trick to play on the poor chap—but it'll be merciful in the long run."

"What's that?"

"Julie's no fool. If he's around the house, and she has the chance to compare him to us and our friends, she'll get things straight for herself."

Margaret was puzzled. "I still don't understand you Darrell."

"Well, to put it with brutal bluntness, if we have him over night and day, day in, day out—if we rub Julie's nose in him so to speak—the glamour's bound to wear thin."

"Well, perhaps... And if we have lots of other young people around, Julie's old friends, members of her own set..."

Whether by design or by accident, Joe refused to fit into their plans. He politely declined to eat dinner with the Hovards more than once or twice a week.

Darrell made discreet inquiries to find out how Joe was handling his job; he was rather annoyed when the contractor told Darrell that if he had any more like Joe to send 'em out.

The crowds of young people Darrell and Margaret had envisioned also failed to materialize. It was a quiet summer. Julie saw a great deal of Cathy and also of Lucia Small, who in an offhand manner let it be known that she had no intention of returning to Radcliffe. Harvard men were dull; she wasn't sure that she wanted a degree in psychology after all.

Lucia was becoming less attractive every year. Her face seemed sallower, her hair more severe. And her disposition had deteriorated with her looks.

She had never been the sort to share confidences, but now she seemed almost secretive. Cathy, softhearted and loyal, worried about Lucia. "I can't understand what's come over her. She almost acts as if we're not her friends!"

"Funny how we change," Julie mused. "We were so different such a short time ago."

"You've never changed," said Cathy affectionately. "You've never been anything but the rattle-brained little twerp you are now."

"I'm wise," said Julie. "Wise with the age-old mystery of Woman."

They were silent a moment. Cathy said with a sigh, "The Masque's Saturday night, and I've still got my costume to do."

"I've got two," said Julie.

"Two?... Oh, yours and Joe's."

Julie nodded.

"He said for sure he'd come?"

"Of course. He has better sense than to disobey me."

"You've got it bad," said Cathy, "sewing already for him." She leaned back and closed her eyes. "I'd just as soon stay home. I know I'm not going to have a good time."

"Sure you will. Think of all the romantic men you'll meet. 'May I have this dance, *mademoiselle*?' Then they'll sweep you up, whirl you breathlessly around the floor—"

"—and all turn out to be Carr."

"Why don't you bust up with him definitely?"

Cathy shrugged. She had been over the ground a hundred times. She could always rely on Carr. If nothing better offered, she might eventually marry him... He wasn't bad-looking—a little inclined to softness around the jowl, but no one was perfect. The Pendrys had plenty of money…If only Carr weren't so spoiled, such a sulky pill when he couldn't get his way.

They fell to talking about their costumes for the Mountainview Masque. It was to be held on the grounds of the new country club, the first of an annual series of costume balls. This year the theme was Black and White Fantasia. The costumes were to reflect nothing but sheer fantasy, and they must be pure black and white.

Julie was sewing herself a skin-tight coverall, black in front, white behind. A casque came up tight over her dark blonde curls, swerving down to a widow's peak at the bridge of her nose. The costume was definitely daring.

"I've never seen anyone look so nearly naked while fully dressed," said Cathy.

"Oh, come now," said Julie. "It's not that bad."

"It's disgraceful. You look like a young imp from hell, a sexy little imp."

"That's exactly what I am."

"Julie!" said Cathy.

Cathy's costume had something of an ancient Egyptian look: a bare-armed tunic of black and white stripes, belted at the waist, with a slit at either side of the skirt. When she walked, her slender olive-skinned legs flashed.

"If it came to a competition for enticing costumes," said Julie, "I hardly think yours would be out of the running."

"Oh nonsense. Everybody knows I have legs."

Lucia came in. She had brought her costume over to show them. It was Spanish — a stiff flat-crowned matador hat, a short black jacket, a white blouse, black breeches, stockings and buckled black shoes. She looked graceless, rigid.

At four, Carr dropped by and refused to answer questions about his costume. He had spent the day at the Republican Headquarters in Paytonville making contacts. Already Pelton Pendry was hinting in the *Herald-Republican* that young blood was needed in Sacramento; that California and the nation needed positive leadership, dynamic thinking.

Carr revealed that he was thinking of going for a master's degree in economics or law at Cal, in preparation for his future.

"As a public servant?" Julie asked jocularly.

Carr made a smiling grimace. "That's a sanctimonious bit of cant that we ought to expunge. A politician has to lead! He can't be worried about popularity! That's why we're in this new-deal, fair-deal, bum-deal mess today! The politicians buying popularity with relief and job-insurance and medical insurance —"

"Come come, Carr," said Lucia. "You're beating a dead horse."

"I think we ought to divide everything up and start over again," said Julie with a perfectly straight face. Carr took a deep breath and leaned forward in his chair. Julie burst out laughing. "Carr, you're really a dear, but you're such fun to tease."

Carr sat back, not quite sure how he felt.

At four-thirty Lucia said she had to be going, and Carr offered to run her home. Lucia accepted; she and Carr departed.

"You know something?" said Julie. "I think Lucia's got a case on Carr."

Cathy looked startled. "She's never done anything about it."

"Maybe we just haven't noticed."

"Somehow," said Cathy, "I just can't see it."

"You're jealous," said Julie. "You're so used to having Carr around you think he's yours."

"No, no," protested Cathy.

"You'll end up marrying him, see if you don't."

Cathy shook her head. "No. But he thinks I will, and that's what makes it so bad." She blushed. "He thinks he's a modern young man, and keeps wanting me to — well, all kinds of things... I guess I'm just not modern."

"Maybe Lucia's modern," said Julie.

Cathy laughed.

Chapter X

Mountainview Masque! It was a wonderful warm evening; breezes smelling of hay and dry odorous weeds rustled through the oaks.

A white canvas pavilion had been erected near the site of the new clubhouse, supported by poles wound with black, red and white ribbon. Booths to right and left functioned as bars; in the center of the pavilion was a tall round stage for the orchestra, like the calliope of a merry-go-round.

Candles furnished the sole illumination: black and white candles in chandeliers made from wine bottles wired together in artistic clusters.

Darrell and Margaret Hovard appeared at eight o'clock with Mrs. Hutson, who was Chairman of the Social Committee. At eight-thirty Julie and Joe arrived in Joe's Plymouth; at nine came the members and their guests.

At nine-thirty the pavilion was crowded; the orchestra, in black and white harlequinade, tuned up and began to play for dancing.

Julie said to Joe, "One of your major shortcomings is that you are hardly a good dancer."

"I admit it," said Joe. He wore black puttees, black boots, a white tunic with black frogs and flaring black epaulettes, and a black and white kepi. Julie called it a space-admiral's uniform.

"Oh, you're not that bad... There's Cathy!" cried Julie.

"Where?"

"Dancing with that man in the black cloak."

"Almost everybody's in a black cloak."

"We're unimaginative in San Giorgio. What do they wear in Boston?"

"Darned if I know."

Julie scrutinized Cathy's dancing partner. "I don't think it's Carr... It's too tall for Carr."

"Carr's over by the bar. In the pirate costume, with the black beard."

"Isn't that odd?" said Julie. "I wonder whatever possessed him to come as a pirate."

"Costumes are symbolic — you dress as something you'd like to be."

"What does that make me? Black in front and white behind."

"That's your character — innocence behind a front of evil and vice."

"What a laugh!"

"Let's go to the bar," said Joe. "Will your father hate me any worse if I buy you a drink?"

"Get Coke highs; then I can pretend it's straight Coke. If anyone bothers to ask."

They found seats; Joe brought over drinks in paper cups. Cathy came over with the man in the black cloak. He said, "Thanks Cathy," and moved off.

A black-bearded pirate, frowning after Black Cloak, joined them. "Who was that?"

"I don't know. I've seen him somewhere."

"I think it's Murray Jones," said Julie. "He walks like Murray."

Carr snapped his fingers at Cathy; she rose. Carr put his arm around her, swung her out on the dance floor with a flourish.

"Poor Cathy," Julie sighed.

"All she's got to do is say no."

"It's not easy for someone like Cathy." A man in tremendous black pantaloons and a billowy white shirt asked Julie to dance; she finished her drink, rose to her feet.

The evening proceeded. Photographers for the *Herald-Republican* moved here and there, pointing glass eyes, discharging gouts of white light, capturing Black and White Fantasia for the Sunday Society Section.

Julie danced with twenty men; she enjoyed herself thoroughly. Joe danced with Lucia and got stuck with her. The bartenders worked unceasingly. At midnight the Masque had taken on life of its own; it was clearly a success.

Unmasking was scheduled for two o'clock. At one, Cathy sought Julie out, where a Cossack was buying her a drink and making arrangements to kiss her. Julie was a trifle high.

"Carr's taking me home," said Cathy.

"Taking you home? Why? The party's just started!"

"He's got a headache."

"Humph." Carr was jealous.

Cathy smiled wanly. "I know. But I'd just as soon. I'll give you a ring in the morning and tell you everything. Good night Julie." She slipped away. The Cossack resumed where he had left off. Julie looked around for Joe; he was nowhere in sight, but presumably with Lucia in the other bar across the pavilion.

The Cossack was placing a new drink in her hands. She noticed with surprise that she had finished her last.

Time passed. The Cossack kissed her. She found herself with still another Coke high. She resolutely put it aside. "You'll get me drunk!" she told the Cossack.

"Money well spent, you lovely."

There was a sudden hush; a rumble, a roar of voices, a rush of feet. Julie craned her neck to see. Into the circle of candlelight came a black pirate. He staggered out on the dance floor. Men and women in black and white gave way. Carr was bloody, his eyes dull and bleared. His mask hung around his neck.

Ralph McDermott, pulling off his own head-dress, pushed over to him. "Carr! What's happened?"

Carr muttered two or three words. Ralph McDermott stood like a post. Then he turned and looked off through the darkness in the direction from which Carr had come.

The Masque dissolved into a group of men and women with frightened faces in foolish costumes.

The orchestra disappeared. The crowd milled, talking in uneasy voices, then trickled to their cars in clots of five or six.

Dr. Federico, Ralph McDermott, and William Biers the district attorney, went in the direction Carr had indicated.

They found the Chrysler sedan half a mile down a dirt road leading to the far end of the country-club property. Biers supported Ralph

McDermott — they did not let him look inside the car — while Dr. Federico made an examination. A glance into the back seat was enough.

He turned slowly away. "There's not a thing we can do." He looked at McDermott. "You'd better go home, Ralph."

Biers said, "Come along, Ralph," and led him away.

Sheriff Clyde Hartmann arrived with his assistants; the horrid task began. The sheriff returned to San Giorgio to take Carr's statement.

The bruise on Carr's head had been cleaned and bandaged. Dr. Harvey was just finishing, and he gave Hartmann permission to ask a few questions. "Try not to keep him too long; he's had an awful shock."

Hartmann nodded. He was a tall, rangy man with silver hair and a handsome deeply lined face.

He said, "I'm sorry I have to intrude on you, Mr. Pendry."

Carr struggled to sit up, then gave up and lay back. He looked pale and drawn; his eyes were like black grapes in two dishes of milk.

"Just what happened, Mr. Pendry?"

"There was somebody in the back..."

"This was when you left the party?"

"That's right...Cathy and I are — well, engaged. I wanted to sit in the car — to park. I drove up the back road. She wasn't feeling well; she wanted to go home." Carr's words came in hoarse spasms. "I started down the road. I looked in the rearview mirror, and saw — this dark shape in the back seat. He must have been down on the floor when we got in." Carr stopped, closed his eyes. Hartmann waited.

Carr spoke with his eyes shut, his head back on the pillow. "I was scared..."

"Of course," said Hartmann.

"I drove for a hundred feet or so; I stopped the car, swung around on the back seat. Cathy turned too; I think she screamed... It was a man in a dark hat and a dark cloak. He had a mask on."

"Did you recognize him at all?"

Carr's eyes opened, roved over the ceiling. "It came so fast — like a nightmare."

"Tell it as you remember it."

"He hit me... I think, twice. Or maybe just once. I can't remember." He was silent a full fifteen seconds. "I don't remember waking up.

Except that I was lying on the floor in the front, and it was very quiet. I sat up, looked in the back. I saw Cathy... And I guess I went a little crazy."

Hartmann nodded. There was a pause.

Carr asked in a weak voice, "Was she attacked?"

Hartmann nodded again. "It looks like it, from the condition of her clothes."

Carr said huskily, "How did she die?"

"Choked," said Hartmann. "He did the work on her face afterward." He consulted his notes. "Was the car locked when you first got in?"

"No."

"Do you have the impression the man was in costume? Or ordinary clothes?"

Carr shook his head. "I don't think it was costume. It couldn't be."

"Why not?"

"I know everyone who was at the party."

"You saw enough to be sure it was no one you knew?"

"No," said Carr. "I know who did it."

Hartmann said in a dry voice, "You do? Who?"

"The same man that killed my sister," said Carr in a cracked voice. "And mutilated her. Robert Struve."

"Robert Struve." Hartmann looked at him thoughtfully. "The name is familiar."

"The boy with the scarred face. Class below me in high school. About five years ago he got in trouble — tried to attack Julie Hovard."

"I remember. Out at the old Martin house. We sent him to Las Lomas. What makes you think it was Struve?"

"He killed my sister," said Carr in a weak voice.

Hartmann was puzzled. "Didn't they convict her husband?"

"He didn't do it."

Hartmann rose to his feet. "Well, I'll look into it."

Joe Treddick telephoned Julie about two o'clock Sunday.

"Oh Joe," cried Julie, "I was hoping you'd call. Won't you come over? I've just got to talk."

"I'll be over."

She was waiting for him on the front steps. "Come around to the back," she said. "I didn't want you to ring the bell."

She took him to the terrace. "Mother and Father are just about crazy. Cathy was part of the family..." She took his hand, held it tight. "Joe, when I think of it — I want to scream — to shut my eyes as hard as I can and scream and scream and scream!"

"I know how you feel."

"I missed you last night — but in the confusion —"

Joe shrugged. "Lucia got tight and I took her home. I got back just about the time the excitement began."

She pressed her head against his shoulder. "Oh, Joe darling, I wish... How could anyone be so horrible?"

"Here comes Carr," said Joe.

Carr wandered in from the Pendry garden, came slowly toward them.

"Golly," said Julie, "does he look a wreck!"

Carr's scalp was swathed in a turban of white bandage, and his face showed hardly more color. He sank into a chair. "I've been down to the sheriff's office," he said in a flat voice.

"Do they have any ideas? Any clues?"

"They found a cloak with blood all over it, in the bushes."

"Carr," said Julie, "don't use that word. Blood. I'll get sick."

Carr nodded grimly, as if he hadn't heard. "I've remembered more of what happened. Do you know what day this is?"

"The twenty-eighth."

"In nine days George Bavonette goes to the gas chamber."

"What's that got to do with Cathy?"

"He's being executed for a crime he didn't commit. Struve killed and hacked up Dean; Struve killed and hacked Cathy."

"But how, Carr?" cried Julie. "How can you be certain?"

"He hit me. I went out... You know how it is when you hear voices in your sleep? When you're not quite able to focus on them?"

"Yes."

"I was dazed. The next thing to being out. I heard this man talking. He said, 'Do you know who I am?' Cathy said something like 'Let go'. Or 'Go away'. He said, 'You don't know who I am, do you? I'm Struve. I'm Robert Struve.'

"She started to cry and scream. I tried to struggle up. He hit me again. I knew he hit me twice."

"You told this to the sheriff?" asked Joe.

"I just got back from telling him." Carr gingerly felt the bandage. "I'm lucky my skull wasn't fractured."

"What did he hit you with?" asked Joe.

"I don't know," said Carr. And he added sarcastically, "He wasn't polite enough to show me."

"Did the sheriff say anything about the cloak? Whose it was?"

"He said he'd trace it. It must be one somebody brought to the Masque."

Julie's hands moved nervously in her lap. "He must have been at the Masque."

Carr shrugged. "Anyone could have come. There wasn't any way to check up. Until two o'clock, of course. All he needed would have been the costume."

"It's weird," said Julie. "It gives me the creeps..."

"You should see the newspapers," said Carr. He rose to his feet. "I'm going to telephone the district attorney in San Francisco. I think he ought to hold up Bavonette's execution." He walked slowly back across the terrace, disappeared through the trees.

Julie sat up straight in the chair, pushed out her chin. "I'm going to stop brooding. I'm just going to get used to it." Tears trickled down her cheek. "Carr's always hated Robert Struve."

"Why?"

"Oh, just one of those high-school situations. Robert had a terrible scar on his face. The bottom of his face was an awful mess..." She hesitated. "I suppose I might as well tell you the whole thing. When I was very little my father let me steer the car. Somehow or other — I don't know whose fault it was — the car ran into him. He was on a motor-scooter. It caught on fire, and burned him terribly. I guess he thought I was responsible." She thought back over the years. "And then when he was a senior — I was a freshman — some of the girls played a mean trick on Robert, at a sorority initiation. They sent me and Dean Pendry and Cathy and Lucia in to kiss Robert. It was part of the initiation. He must have caught on to what was going on. I suppose it hurt him... Well," she said blushing, "when I went in, he grabbed me. The other kids didn't hear me yelling... In fact, Sheriff Hartmann was raiding the place." She arranged her skirt over her knees. "Well, anyway they caught him and charged him with attack and assault and battery, and sent him to reform school... And that's the last we heard of him." She said as an afterthought, "His mother died while he was in reform school."

They sat quietly. Julie suddenly beat her knees with her fists. "I wish I were a million miles away..."

Carr came back around the swimming pool, his face flushed and angry. He sat down. "They think I'm a crank."

The maid came out of the house. "Miss Julie, Sheriff Hartmann wants to talk to you."

"Oh... Will you bring him out here, please?"

Hartmann came sauntering out, looking more like a prosperous bond salesman than a sheriff. "Hello, Julie... Carr..."

"Sheriff Hartmann—Joe Treddick," said Julie.

Carr burst out, "I just called Maynard in San Francisco. The District Attorney. He politely told me to mind my own business."

Hartmann nodded. "He couldn't stay an execution merely because a similar crime is committed elsewhere. Bavonette was found guilty in a jury trial, sentenced to death. There's no new evidence bearing on that trial."

Carr suddenly subsided. "I've done all I can. If they kill him, it's on their own heads."

The sheriff shrugged. "Well, I'm afraid it's outside of my province." He looked at Julie. "I'd like to ask a few questions."

"Of course."

"Did Cathy have any new boy friends?"

"Nothing serious... She was always meeting new men, naturally, but none of them meant anything to her."

"Anyone pay her special attention? Abnormal attentions?"

"No," said Julie. "I'm sure not."

"How about at the party? Did she dance with any strangers, make any dates?"

"Of course not!" snapped Carr.

The sheriff rose to his feet. "Can you think of anything that might throw light on the matter? Any of you?"

Julie shook her head.

"Sorry," said Joe Treddick.

"Well," said Hartmann, "if you do, let me know."

He made a graceful departure. Carr muttered passionately, "That's what comes of electing a playboy for sheriff... For two cents, I'd — I'd..."

"Run for sheriff?" asked Joe.

Carr glared. "This isn't any time to be flippant."

Lucia came through the house. "I thought I'd find you all here."

She was wearing a simple dark green cotton dress, her dark hair hung loosely; her face looked clean and fresh, as if she'd just washed it in cold water.

Julie said, "Lucia, it's a sin looking so pretty at a time like this."

Lucia sat down in one of the white iron chairs. There was a glow in her eyes, a flush to her skin.

"Thanks for taking me home," she said to Joe. "I don't know what on earth got into me."

"Some call it alcohol," said Carr sourly.

Lucia tittered. Julie looked at her curiously.

"I don't usually drink so much. It must have been awfully early."

"About one," said Joe.

Lucia looked from face to face. "Any news?"

Julie shrugged. "Carr says it was Robert Struve that hit him."

"Robert Struve!" Lucia was astonished. She twisted in her chair, looked Carr up and down. "Carr's got Robert Struve on the brain."

Carr looked away, controlling his retort.

Lucia said, "Why should Robert Struve go to all that trouble? Why should he single out Cathy?"

"He's a maniac," said Carr. "But they'll catch him..."

"The only time Cathy had anything to do with him," Julie mused, "was that awful Tri-Gamma initiation."

Lucia's eyes widened, then narrowed. She licked her lips. "I was there — and you too, Julie. And Dean."

"Dean's dead," said Carr curtly. "Also Cathy... Neither one of you better go anywhere alone."

Julie said nervously, "Oh, Carr, it's ridiculous."

"Yeah," said Carr sardonically. "It is, isn't it?"

Joe rose to his feet. "I think I'll be on my way."

Julie went with him out to his car.

"I don't know what she sees in that guy," said Carr. "He doesn't have brains or money or family or looks."

Lucia glanced at him appraisingly. "Girls are funny."

"You can say that again," muttered Carr.

CHAPTER XI

ON TUESDAY MORNING, the day of Cathy's funeral, Julie received an anonymous letter in a square white envelope. She opened it, pulled out a piece of white cardboard, apparently cut by hand to fit the envelope.

She sat at her desk and studied the envelope. The address had been stamped in purple ink, with rubber type obtainable in any stationery store.

Slowly, she read the words neatly stamped in thin purple ink:

> IF ONLY YOU KNEW WHAT I KNOW.
> WHAT A JOKE.

Julie was perplexed, and more than a little frightened.

Who had written the letter?

Which of the faces she knew concealed this strange soul?

What did the letter mean? 'If only you knew what I know.' Something was going on that she ought to know about. The person who wrote the letter knew but wouldn't tell her. The person must hate her!

Julie shuddered. Never in her pampered young life had the idea occurred to her that someone seriously disliked her.

Here was the evidence. Someone detested her.

What to do! Show the letter to her father? No. He would take the letter, reassure her with bluff generalities. That wasn't what Julie wanted. The letter was alarming, but it was exciting too. She wanted to know who had written it; to watch the person; to detect the roiling in the superficial skin of friendship. Julie shivered with a strange new delight.

She lay on the bed looking at the letter. Never again would she be the same feckless Julie Hovard. A phrase came out of the past: 'rattle-brained little twerp'. Cathy had said that.

Cathy... If only Cathy could come back, if only she could tell what had happened.

Julie jumped up, went downstairs and called Lucia.

"This is Julie, Lucia."

"You sound pretty low."

"I am... How would you like to go for a ride?"

"I've got other things on my mind," said Lucia. "Such as the anonymous letter that came this morning."

"You got one? So did I! What did yours say?"

Lucia hesitated. "Are you going to be home?"

"Yes."

"I'll drop by."

Julie hung up; as she turned away the phone rang.

"Julie? Carr."

"Hello, Carr."

"Er — how are you?"

"Okay. How are you?"

"Oh — just as usual. Five foot ten of solid muscle."

"Including the skull."

"That's not a nice thing to say." Carr sounded arch; Julie wondered what he thought he was up to. Flirtation? Today was Cathy's funeral. She decided she was doing him an injustice.

"Carr — something's worrying me."

"What?"

"I got an anonymous letter."

Carr sounded surprised — and oddly relieved. "You did? So did I!"

"And so did Lucia... What does yours say?"

"Oh, well." Carr sounded vague and distant, as if he had moved back from the phone. "It's a kind of threatening letter."

"Well, what does it say?"

There was a pause, a crackling of paper — " 'I hold two lives in my careless hands.' "

"Golly."

"What's yours?"

" 'If only you knew what I know. What a joke.' "

Carr was silent; there was only the hum of the telephone.

"Carr?" said Julie. "Who would write something like that…Carr?"

"I don't know…" A moment later he said briskly: "I'll drop by and take you to the funeral."

"Joe is coming."

"Oh. Well, I'll see you there."

When Lucia arrived Julie led the way up to her room. "I haven't said anything to my folks about this thing…They'd get all excited."

"I haven't either."

"Carr got one too."

"He did? Did he tell you what was in it?"

" 'I hold two lives in my hands.' "

Lucia sat down. "And what did yours say?"

Julie tossed it to her. Lucia read it. Her face twitched. She gave it back.

"Let's see yours," said Julie.

Lucia slowly bent over her handbag. "It's not nice — it's not like yours. It's obscene."

"Oh, come, Lucia. Let's see the silly thing."

Lucia passed it over.

Julie compressed her lips. "It *is* nasty…"

Lucia looked out the window. "There's a maniac loose."

Julie snorted. "That's no news." She appraised Lucia's clothes: a black afternoon dress, a black hat. "Is that what you're wearing to the funeral?"

Lucia nodded.

"I don't have anything black — except my faille suit. It's a rag, but a funeral isn't supposed to be a social event." She looked up at her wall clock. "Golly — I'd better get started. Do you want to wait, Lucia? We can go together. Joe's coming by."

"All right."

An hour later Joe rang the bell. Julie opened the door.

"Come on in, Joe. Mother thinks we'd better all go together."

Joe hesitated. "Maybe I'd better go ahead."

Julie took his arm. "Oh, nonsense. Come in." She led him into the living room where Lucia was waiting.

"Look what I got this morning," said Julie. She handed him her letter.

Joe read it without comment.

"Aren't you surprised?" asked Julie.

"No. I got one too."

"You did! What did it say? Do you have it with you?"

"No. I threw it away."

"Well, what did it say? Don't keep us in suspense."

Joe grinned painfully. "It said that you'd never marry me. Never, never, never."

Julie was indignant. "Isn't that awful!"

Margaret Hovard came downstairs; Darrell Hovard met them in front with the Cadillac and they drove to the funeral.

Joe stayed to dinner; afterward he and Julie went out on the terrace. They sat in a lawn swing, rocking idly back and forth.

"Joe," said Julie, "what do you think about this business?"

"You mean — Cathy? And the letters?"

"Yes."

Joe took his time answering. "I'm not sure just what I do think."

Julie knit her brows. "What's so puzzling is the Robert Struve angle. I can understand his killing Cathy — but why should he send out anonymous letters?"

Joe smiled grimly. "The person who wrote the letters didn't do the killing."

"Why do you say that?"

"I've got a very strong hunch who wrote the letters."

"Who?"

"Lucia."

Julie looked at him in astonishment. "Lucia? But Joe — why should Lucia write letters like that? And the awful one she got herself!"

"What did it say?"

Julie blushed. "It was — well, it wasn't nice. It said that — well, that she'd make a good prostitute."

Joe nodded. "Lucia's a frustrated old maid."

"But Joe — she's only twenty!"

"Some girls are old maids at six."

"Do you think she knows anything — about Cathy? What time did you take her home?"

"About twelve-thirty. I got back just in time to see Carr stagger into the pavilion. And I was with her an hour before I took her home."

"Then she *couldn't* have known anything about Cathy. You're all wrong Joe. Someone else wrote those letters. Why not Robert Struve?"

"I suppose anything's possible." Joe rose to his feet. "I'd better go before your father chases me away with a horsewhip."

Julie said good night to him on the porch, and stood watching the red taillight disappear around the curve of the road. She turned to go back inside, but paused, and went listlessly out on the front lawn. The night was dark and clear; the stars glimmered, clean, remote, dispassionate…What was up there, among those far suns? If the spirits of the dead persisted, perhaps they might drift out there, out among the stars… Her skin crawled as she thought of Cathy. Pale, lonesome Cathy, wandering among those far black places…

As she turned to go back into the house headlights came up the driveway. Julie recognized the Jaguar. She sighed; Carr was the last person she wanted to talk to. But she couldn't escape.

"McDermott's hired a detective," he told Julie. "I've just come from his house."

"That's — that's very interesting," Julie said weakly.

Carr nodded grimly. "But he's got to get on the ball. Today's the thirteenth. On July seventh they execute Bavonette."

"But Carr —"

Carr interrupted in a hard voice: "Not that I care a tinker's damn for Bavonette. I just hate to see him paying for Struve's fun." He patted Julie on the shoulder. "Well, old girl, Cathy's gone; it looks like you and I are about what's left of the old gang."

"I'm going in Carr," said Julie.

"Oh? Wouldn't you like to come for a ride? Let the fresh air blow away the vapors?"

"No, Carr."

"Just as you like…Good night."

Chapter XII

Julie sat at her desk, looked at the envelope, afraid to open it, afraid of what it might say.

The address, stamped in the purple ink, looked back at her:

MISS JULIE HOVARD
10 JAMAICA TERRACE
SAN GIORGIO, CALIFORNIA.

Julie touched the envelope; was it really Lucia? She opened the letter.

CATHY IS QUITE DEAD.
I KNOW WHO QUIETED HER. MAYBE YOU
WILL BE QUIETED TOO.

"Hello Julie!" Lucia was wearing blue denim shorts, a red blouse, moccasins. Her hair was loose, she wore no lipstick; she looked rather pretty.

"Julie," said Lucia breathlessly, "can you guess what came this morning?"

"Yes," said Julie.

Judge Small came into the room, a tall stern old man, deaf as a post, with gaunt cheeks, a brush of white hair, a minatory eye of which Julie had always been in awe. He wore a baggy gray twill suit, with round-toed black shoes, a heavy gold watch chain. Julie had never seen him otherwise, morning or night.

"Good morning Judge," she called politely.

Judge Small nodded. "Good morning." He cleared his throat raspily. "You're the Hovard child, aren't you?"

Lucia said, "Of course, Father — you've known Julie for years. She's in college now."

Judge Small nodded jerkily, stamped off to his library.

Lucia looked at her sidelong. "What's the trouble?"

"I got another letter this morning."

"I did too. That's what I started to tell you!"

Julie nodded. "I know you did." The seed of suspicion had suddenly become certainty. In the flicker of an eyelid Lucia was a different person, and all the qualities Julie had known and respected had to be re-interpreted.

Julie set her mouth into a thin line of resolution. "Let's go up to your room, where we can talk." She started up the gloomy echoing stairs.

Lucia's bedroom was a large airy chamber at the southeast corner of the house. The ceiling was twelve feet high, festooned with gilt ornamental plaster. Six tall windows, veiled in lace and apple-green draperies, rose almost to the ceiling, with window seats below. The furniture was rather elaborate — antiques of a period Julie could put no name to. The room smelled faintly of sandalwood, and the impeccable tidiness jarred on Julie after the cheerful disorder of her own room.

Lucia followed Julie slowly through the door, her eyes narrow with calculation. "What's all the mystery?"

"Certainly not the letters," said Julie.

Lucia said crisply, "What about the letters?"

"I want to know one thing, Lucia. Did you write them?"

Lucia laughed. "What a question Julie!"

"Did you? Or not?"

"Of course not. Do you think that I'm — Julie!" she cried in anxiety as Julie ran to her tall desk, pulled down the flap. Tucked neatly into a pigeonhole was a printing set. In another were white cards. In still another were square white envelopes.

Lucia slammed the desk shut, turned and slapped Julie's face. Her eyes glittered.

Julie laughed. "So you know who killed Cathy, Lucia. Who?"

"Wouldn't you like to know?" panted Lucia.

"I thought Joe took you home early."

"What I know, I know. Now get out of this house! I don't ever want to see you again!"

"It's not as easy as that, Lucia. You've been writing vicious threatening letters. I don't know whether it's a criminal offense or not — but we can ask your father."

Lucia sat down in a chair, tears forming in her eyes. They were tears of fury.

"I want to know what you mean," said Julie. " 'Cathy is quite dead. I know who quieted her. You may be quieted too.' "

Lucia's mouth twisted. "You think you're smart, don't you?"

"Who killed Cathy, Lucia? If you know, you ought to tell the police... Is it someone we know?"

Lucia smiled. "Maybe."

"Is it Robert Struve?"

"Maybe."

"Well — do you know for sure?"

"Yes," said Lucia. "I would say so."

"How did you find out?"

"I used my common sense."

"And you think that whoever did it might do it again?"

Lucia shrugged. "I don't know." The two girls sat in silence. Lucia stared into the air as if listening to secret voices. She began to speak in a soft monotone, not addressing Julie, but speaking for Julie to hear.

"I'm twenty years old. I've never let a man touch me — and I've gained what? Not a thing. No one likes me or respects me; they think I'm cold... But I don't care any more. I'm going to do what I want to do — and I'm not going to give a damn."

"Lucia," said Julie breathlessly, "listen. I'm your friend..."

"You're my friend? You're nobody's friend but stuck-up little Julie Hovard's."

"That's not true!" cried Julie, tears coming to her eyes. "Think, Lucia! Just think! Suppose you know who killed poor Cathy — and suppose whoever did it knows you know! Think what might happen!"

Lucia smiled. "I've taken care of that. I've made it clear. He'd just better be careful." She jumped to her feet. "And as for you, Julie Hovard — I hate you! I don't care what happens to you!"

"Okay," said Julie. "We know where we stand. But — if I wanted to find out who killed Cathy — where would I start?"

"It's in the paper. In Sunday's paper, the society section. Right in front of your nose. But you'll never see it, not in a million years. I could show it to you and you still wouldn't see it."

"All right," said Julie, "show it to me."

"Oh, get out of here," said Lucia. She flung herself on the bed.

Julie said irresolutely, "Lucia — if you've got something on your mind, maybe we could talk it over..."

Lucia turned her head, and they stared at each other.

"Cathy was killed!" cried Julie. "Don't you understand? She's dead!"

Lucia turned her head away. "I wish I had been there to watch."

Julie ran out the door, down the long dark steps. At the newel post she stopped, and looked into the library. Judge Small lay asleep in a tremendous black leather chair.

Julie drove slowly back to town. She found a parking place, went into the city hall, around the cool corridors to the sheriff's office.

Sheriff Hartmann was not in, the woman at the desk said.

"Do you know when he'll be back?"

"As soon as he gets a week's quota of wetbacks."

"Will you tell him Julie Hovard wants to see him?"

"All right, Miss Hovard. I'll leave the message."

Julie wanted company; someone to talk to, someone to soothe her.

Cathy was dead.

She thought, I'll take a run up to Mountainview and see how things are coming along. As she passed the contractor's shack she noticed one of the dump trucks standing idle. She parked, jumped out of the car and ran into the office.

"I want to see Joe Treddick; can you tell me where he is?"

A tall man in dusty suntans looked her over. "Search me. He quit this morning."

"Quit! What for?"

"That I don't know... He just up and quit."

Julie gunned the convertible back to town. She was very angry. Joe had no business to do a thing like that without consulting her. Well, he could go chase himself... Somehow the way home led past the Fair Oaks Guest House.

The old Plymouth sedan was nowhere in sight.

Julie parked, walked up to the screen door, rang the bell. A middle-aged woman with straggly gray hair appeared on the other side of the screen.

"I'm looking for Joe Treddick," said Julie.

"You've missed him by half an hour."

"You mean he's — moved out?"

"Yes, ma'am."

"Did he — leave an address?"

The woman peered sharply through the screen. "No, he didn't."

"Very well," said Julie wearily. "Thanks very much."

She drove home, feeling very low. Joe's car was in the driveway. Joe was just coming out of the house.

Julie tried hard to control her face. "Joe!"

He came over to the convertible. "Hello Julie. I was afraid I was going to miss you."

"Joe — where are you going?" She took his hand.

"I've quit, Julie. I'm leaving San Giorgio."

"But why?"

He smiled. "I don't like what's happening around here."

Julie looked at the house. Very probably her mother was watching from one of the windows. "Get in, Joe. Let's go for a ride. I want to talk to you."

He got in; Julie drove around the circle, down to the highway, and away from San Giorgio.

"Tell me the truth, Joe."

He was slow in answering. "I should never have come up here in the first place Julie."

"Did you get another letter this morning?"

"Yes."

"What did it say?"

"I'd rather not go into that."

Tears were welling up behind Julie's eyes. "I got a letter too. You can read mine." She pulled over to the side of the road, opened the glove compartment, gave him the letter.

He read it in silence.

Julie said, "I went over and saw Lucia. We—had a showdown. You were right. She's been writing the letters."

Joe nodded.

"I don't want you to go, Joe! Suppose Lucia was right—suppose somebody 'quieted' me."

"That's not too likely."

"Why not? Suppose Robert Struve is in San Giorgio? Suppose he *is* a maniac?"

"If he killed Cathy, and he's got any sense at all, he'll get the hell out of San Giorgio."

"Joe—would you desert a sinking ship?" And they both laughed.

"I've quit my job."

"We'll go up there right now and un-quit."

"But Julie!"

"Suppose you read in the paper that my corpse had been found. Victim of a sex-mutilation murder. Would you ever forgive yourself?"

He was clenching and unclenching his hands. "I don't know whether I would or not."

She kissed his cheek. "Oh Joe, the world's such a terrible place!" She looked up into his face. "Tell me you'll take care of me, Joe."

"Yes," said Joe. "I'll take care of you."

She closed her eyes. Joe hesitated a second, then kissed her. Julie put her arms up for another. They separated slowly.

"Right in broad daylight," said Julie. "Sometimes I wish I weren't so affectionate... Lucia's stored hers up. And now it's broken loose on her," Julie mused. "I just hope she doesn't get into trouble." She rapped the steering wheel with her knuckles. "That reminds me."

"What?"

"Well—" Julie hesitated. "She said I could find who killed Cathy by looking at Sunday's society page."

"Yeah?" Joe pondered a moment. "Let's go look."

They sat close together on the couch in the Hovard living room, heads bent over the *Herald-Republican* society section.

"She said I'd never see it — not in a million years," said Julie. "And I guess she's right, because we've been looking ten minutes and I don't see a thing."

Joe squinted up and down the page. "Let's give it one more try. From the headline down."

– EVENT OF THE SEASON –
MOUNTAINVIEW MASQUE.

"It was an event all right," said Joe.

Once more, they examined the photographs. There were eight of these, arranged around a central box of text describing the most noteworthy of the costumes and those who wore them.

Julie took the paper, bent over it. "There's Mother and Father in this picture —" she pointed "— and that thing there is my leg; I'm sitting right behind the woman in the snake-goddess hat... Here's you and Lucia at the bar."

Joe took the paper. He and Lucia were standing a little aside from the black and white throng. Lucia had her head tilted to the side; Joe, by a trick of reproduction, looked somber and heavy.

"Why are you so glum?" asked Julie.

Joe shrugged. "I was just taking her home... We were pushing over to the door."

"She looks a little silly," said Julie.

Joe nodded. "She was fairly tight — but not too tight."

Julie looked up in sudden speculation. "Not too tight — for what?"

Joe grinned. "Gentlemen never talk."

"Oh. So there's something to talk about."

Her tone surprised Joe; she seemed suddenly years older. "No... Nothing very much. I just got the notion she was willing."

"And so you parked?" Joe shook his head. Julie's voice was skeptical. "Lucia's nice when she isn't looking down her nose at something."

"I've seen worse."

Julie sniffed. "Oh well. If you really admire Lucia..."

Joe tossed the newspaper to the table. "I don't really."

"But you parked with her on the way home."

"How could I park with Lucia and get back to the Masque in half an hour?"

"You left earlier."

"I didn't. But I'd have a hell of a time proving it."

Julie picked up the paper. "One last look."

"I think Lucia's more than a little nuts," said Joe.

"Maybe. But she was so darn triumphant!... Look, maybe this is it."

"What?"

Julie pointed. "This man." She pointed to a shape on the dance floor.

"What about him?"

"He's got his mask on. He danced with Cathy several times. No one knew who he was. No one does yet."

"A man danced with Cathy. So what?"

"He might be Robert Struve."

Joe laughed. "You're letting Robert Struve hypnotize you."

"Somebody killed her. Nobody else had any reason to."

"But what reason could Struve have? That's something I've never got straight."

Julie sighed. "It's a long story. I only know what Cathy told me... It all goes back to that awful Tri-Gamma initiation."

Joe waited.

"Cathy and Lucia and Dean went into the room. To kiss Robert. They thought he was passed out — drunk — and made some silly cracks. Nothing serious — but I suppose they were rather mean. Enough to make Robert hate them all."

"That was years ago. It sounds far-fetched."

"Cathy and Dean both had their faces cut up. Just where Robert's face was so awful. And Carr heard him — heard what he said to Cathy."

Joe tossed the paper to the coffee table. "I've got an idea."

"What?"

"Lucia says she knows what's going on."

Julie regarded him quizzically. "And your idea is to take Lucia out for a ride, and park."

"It was just an idea," said Joe.

"You're full of ideas." Julie kicked at the newspaper. "She'd be lording it over me for years. Worse than she does now."

"She's just jealous."

"I'd rather have her jealous of me than me jealous of her."

"You've never been jealous of anyone in your life."

"Oh, yes I have... But I'd never tell you of whom."

Joe rose to his feet. "I think I'll be going."

"Okay," said Julie. "But before you do another thing, you go and get your job back."

"All right," said Joe. "If you say so."

"I say so. Now give me a kiss."

Chapter XIII

Out at the Turrets, twilight had come. The sun was twenty minutes gone; the sky was a smear of orange into which the old gables cut notches of absorbent black. The trees around the house had collected a brood of shadows.

The house was quiet. Judge Small sat in the library with Chapman's *Doctrines of Freehold* on his lap. His head lolled back; he was dozing. The maid had set out a pre-bedtime collation and gone home.

Lucia was up in her room. She lay on the bed, leafing slowly through the pages of a large book in front of her. It was the San Giorgio High School yearbook, the year of her graduation. She turned the pages and the familiar faces appeared, passed, and were gone.

On one page she lingered, looking into Cathy McDermott's face. It smiled out, innocently confident. Lucia made a bitter sardonic sound in her throat, a comment on the unpredictability of life, tinged faintly with satisfaction. On the opposite page was Dean Pendry, with head flung back to display the profile, the tempestuous hair.

She flicked the pages over — one after the other — to the S's. Lucia Small. And Lucia stared at the picture. Her hair — she had worn it drawn tightly back from her face. Her mouth was pressed into a prim little smile meaning nothing.

"I'm not like that!" said Lucia between her teeth. "I'm not like that!"

She turned pages quickly. The junior group pictures: Julie Hovard. Egotistical little smart-aleck, so gay and assured. Lucia thought of the Tri-Gamma initiation, nodded with a bitter smile. Lucia had never been under any illusions about that. And Julie passing it off so nonchalantly!

Lucia jumped to her feet, went to the full-length mirror on the inside of her closet door. She stood looking at herself.

I'm pretty! she thought defiantly. She put her hands to her waist, turned this way and that. I'm fine-boned, she thought. I have a patrician body, small breasts, lithe hips.

She slipped out of her clothes.

The doorway behind her opened. Slowly, an inch, two inches, three... A man stood watching. Lucia picked up her skirt — and a quiver of the air, a mental tremor disturbed her. She looked at the door.

The man stepped into the room. She opened her mouth, but managed no more than a hoarse croak.

"Take it easy, take it easy... You're lovely this way."

"What do you want!" Lucia gasped. "Get out of here!"

"But I just came." He looked her over. "You shouldn't have sent so many letters, Lucia."

"Maybe I shouldn't have." Lucia's voice was strangely free from panic. "I've written other letters, too. They'll be mailed if anything happens to me."

He came toward her. Lucia slid into his arms, pressed against his chest.

Downstairs old Judge Small stirred, yawned. He lay quiet, his head back on the soft old black leather, his throat corrugated and rough. He reached out for his book, put on his glasses, resumed his reading. He turned a page, nodding now and then.

A sound from somewhere? Judge Small blinked, looked around the library. Nothing seemed amiss.

Upstairs the man went softly to the door, looked out; no one in sight. He slipped along the hall to the bathroom, locked himself in, washed with care.

Downstairs in the library, Judge Small levered himself to his feet, ambled into the dining room, inspected the buffet through the bifocal section of his spectacles. He served himself grated cabbage and carrot, a cold boiled egg, a handful of crackers. He seated himself, ate.

When he had finished, he yawned, rose heavily, stood a moment looking through the arch into the hall. It was the gleam of the library light on the waxed hardwood floor which apparently had caught his attention. He stared vacantly for ten seconds, twenty seconds, sucking a shred of cabbage from his teeth.

Still sucking, he went forward to his private elevator, settled himself, punched the button. The car rose up the shaft.

In Lucia's room, the man felt the whir of the motor. He paused. The whir stopped, and a moment later the window of the north turret glowed yellow. The judge was secure in his study, until midnight or later.

The man, now wearing gloves, went to Lucia's escritoire. He turned the key, lowered the panel, explored the various nooks and pigeon-holes. He found nothing to interest him.

He locked the desk, began a search of the room. His leisure was almost insolent, as was his unconcern whether he found anything or not. Lucia might have sought to protect herself — perhaps a letter to be mailed to the authorities — but what of it? What could she prove? What could anyone prove?

In the drawer of the bedside table he found a clipping from the *Herald-Republican* society page. A photograph. He examined it, shrugged, folded and tucked it in his pocket.

He paused by the bed for a last look at Lucia.

He compressed his lips, shook his head. He backed away, paused at the door, glanced around the room like a gardener inspecting a plot. Then he switched off the light, left the room and departed the house.

The long dark night passed. The room was quiet. Dawn came, silver light entered the room; then yellow strands of sunlight penetrated the curtains.

At ten there were brisk footsteps in the hall. The door opened wide. When she was able, the maid called Sheriff Hartmann, bypassing deaf old Judge Small.

By nightfall San Giorgio seethed with sensation. Two mutilation murders in the week, a maniac at large! Sheriff Hartmann felt blind, baffled, helpless. He had no suspects to question, no leads, no idea of where or how to begin. A single course of inquiry presented itself, stemming from Carr Pendry's half-dazed identification of Robert Struve. It was a poor piece of evidence. But it was a lead, and he had no others.

✷

About eleven o'clock Carr Pendry appeared at the Hovards' with a stranger — a small thin man with a bank-clerk face, wearing incongruously sporty clothes: a chocolate-brown gabardine suit, a narrow dark-brown knit tie, yellow-brown shoes.

The maid answered the bell; Margaret Hovard came curiously to see who was calling. "Oh, it's you Carr."

"Hello, Mrs. Hovard. This is Mr. Brevis. Mr. Brevis is a private detective."

"You're the man Mr. McDermott engaged?"

Brevis nodded. "I'd appreciate it, Mrs. Hovard, if you mentioned my connection with this case to no one."

"Naturally not."

"I'd like to talk to your daughter, if you'll permit me."

"As you wish," said Mrs. Hovard. "Though I don't see how she can help you." Margaret went to the foot of the stairs. "Julie!"

Julie came down from her room.

"This is Mr. Brevis, dear," said Margaret. "He's a detective, and he wants to talk to you."

Julie nodded. She stood looking at him.

"I think it would be better to talk privately," said Brevis.

Before Margaret could protest, Julie said, "Let's go out here on the terrace." She led the way, Brevis followed.

Julie and Brevis talked almost an hour, then joined Margaret and Carr.

"Well, Brevis," Carr said bluffly, "did you learn anything?"

"I think I have a general idea of the situation," said Brevis.

Carr cleared his throat. "Was Julie able to help you in any way?"

Brevis shrugged. "We discussed the case..."

Brevis stood in the front office of the Las Lomas Detention Home.

"Well, well," he said. "That's very interesting, but —"

"It's all I can tell you, and it's exactly what I told your office over the telephone. I spoke to the sheriff myself. Sheriff Hartmann." She eyed him quizzically, a stout, intelligent woman in a brown tweed suit. "Peculiar they'd send you down and then call, too."

Brevis made a noncommittal gesture. "Perhaps there's someone here who knew Robert Struve particularly well? A matron, perhaps?"

The woman flipped pages in a ledger, ran her finger down a list of names. "That would be Mrs. Fador." She picked up a phone, dialed.

"Mrs. Fador, please... Mrs. Fador, this is Anna. There's a man here from San Giorgio, making inquiries about Robert Struve. He wants to speak to someone who knew Robert well... Dr. O'Brien. Thank you." She pressed down the bar, released it, dialed again.

She held a brief conversation with Dr. O'Brien, then made a sign to Brevis. "Down the corridor, turn to the right, cross the courtyard. Ask for Dr. O'Brien. He knew Robert Struve as well as anyone here."

Dr. O'Brien's office was a large room cluttered with miscellaneous furniture: odd bookcases, a big table, chairs. O'Brien sat in a swivel chair, with books on one side of him, a basket of papers on the other. His face was sunburned a fire-red, and glistened with oil.

"Excuse me for not getting up," he said to Brevis. "I fell asleep in the sun this morning. Stupid thing to do... Won't you sit down?"

Brevis slipped into a chair beside the desk. "My name is Brevis. I'm a detective."

"Oh, yes," said O'Brien. "With the San Giorgio police."

"I'm afraid there's been a misunderstanding," said Brevis. "I am a private detective." He showed O'Brien his credentials. O'Brien became quizzical. "Oh. Just what's the trouble?"

Brevis straightened. "Well, sir, frankly, I'm rather at sea. I'm confused by the whole situation; I thought perhaps you'd be able to straighten me out." O'Brien relaxed in his chair and frowned thoughtfully.

"Robert Struve, eh? Exactly what kind of trouble has he got himself in?"

"Perhaps you've read about the San Giorgio mutilation murders."

"Oh, yes," said O'Brien. "Do you think — I mean, you have some idea that Struve is responsible?"

Brevis shook his head. "That's what I'm here to find out — if there's any chance that Struve could be the murderer."

O'Brien shrugged, and winced at the pain. "It's hard to say. Robert — well, there's a great deal to him — an extraordinary persistence, direction. But I've never been quite sure just where this direction led."

"What sort of boy was he?"

O'Brien rose gingerly to his feet, moved across the room to a filing cabinet, rummaged through the contents, returned with a manila folder. "Here's the folder on Robert Struve," he said. "Here's his picture — before plastic surgery, of course."

Brevis took the photograph. "Mmmph... Not a pretty sight."

"No," said O'Brien. "As nasty a wad of tissue as I've ever seen. Luckily, it lifted clear. They did a splendid job of repair."

"Do you have a picture of Struve after the operation?"

Dr. O'Brien looked uncomfortable. He laughed. "Struve was photographed upon his entrance, as per regulations. After the operation, no one had the responsibility to photograph him... I guess it just never got done."

Brevis studied the photograph. "The change in his face presumably changed his character?"

O'Brien shrugged. "It certainly affected his behavior."

"Well, let me put it this way. Can you see Robert Struve nursing a grudge for five years, then performing horrible crimes to satisfy this grudge?"

"I can't give you an honest answer. I've always thought of him as a lad with a terrible burden. I don't think he ever had a childhood. His mother was a rather weak woman who apparently made him the man of the family at the age of nine. When he left us — well, I confess I didn't know how he'd make out. I recommended his discharge because I felt that the Army would be much better therapy than the Home."

"He enlisted?"

"No. His draft number came up. We had the option of releasing him to the Army or holding him here till he was twenty-one. We chose the Army. There seemed to be no question of moral turpitude; we felt the boy was the victim of circumstances, and he was inducted on this basis."

"Do you know where he reported for induction?"

"Sacramento, I believe."

"I see... May I trouble you for Robert's fingerprint classification?"

O'Brien tossed across Robert Struve's file card.

Brevis made a quick note. "You've been very helpful, Doctor."

"Perhaps," said Dr. O'Brien, "you'll tell me just how Robert Struve is involved in this affair."

"Frankly, Doctor, it's what I'm trying to find out."

"I see...Well, it's always disturbing to hear of our boys getting in trouble."

"Don't misunderstand me Doctor. He's not in trouble. There's only a hint that he's connected so far. It's quite possible that I'm proving him innocent."

Dr. O'Brien seemed to lose interest in the subject. "Well, I can't tell you anything more. Some of the boys we get to know pretty well. Others we don't. Robert Struve was one of those we didn't."

Brevis returned to San Giorgio two days later and drove to the San Giorgio Building and Loan Association.

McDermott was sitting behind his desk, hands folded on the green blotter. Brevis came quietly into the room.

McDermott motioned to a chair. "What did you find out?"

"Nothing conclusive," said Brevis. He reached in his pocket, produced a notebook. "What there is took some ungodly digging to get. I've been to half a dozen different bureaus and record offices. I've cost you thirty-five dollars in bribes."

McDermott waited. Brevis consulted the notes which he already knew by heart.

"On January 12, 1950, Robert Struve was inducted into the Army. He was assigned to the Engineers, and shipped overseas — first to the Philippines, where he was promoted to corporal; then to Japan, then to Korea.

"In July, 1951, his unit was ordered into front-line duty. On November 1, 1951, Corporal Robert Struve was killed in action, along with his entire platoon."

"Well, well," said McDermott. "There's no possibility of a mistake?"

"I saw the official list."

McDermott rubbed his forehead, sank back into his chair.

"I ran into something else," said Brevis casually.

McDermott looked at him vacantly. "Eh?"

"As I reported to you, Struve's entire platoon were casualties. I believe a mortar shell fell among them. There was a single exception, a man who was not killed, but captured by the Chinese."

"Well?"

The telephone rang.

"Excuse me," said McDermott. He lifted the receiver. "Hello?"

"This is Carr Pendry, Mr. McDermott. I've got some news. I thought I'd better let you know."

"What's the news?"

"I've just come from talking to Sheriff Hartmann. He's traced Robert Struve."

McDermott looked across the room to Brevis. "Where is he?"

"He's dead."

"Oh, yes. I knew that already."

"Oh." Carr came to a lame halt. "Well, I thought I'd let you know."

McDermott hung up, reached for his checkbook. "How much do I owe you?"

Brevis compressed his lips. "There's one more item of information which may interest you."

McDermott leaned back. "Go ahead."

"One man from Struve's platoon escaped death, as I said."

"Yes. What about him?"

"It may be no more than a farfetched coincidence — but isn't the chap who goes around with Julie Hovard named Joe Treddick?"

"Why yes," said McDermott. "I believe so."

"That was the name of the man who survived from Robert Struve's platoon. Joe Treddick."

"You don't say..." McDermott reflected for a moment. "What do you think?"

"Personally, I think it's a matter for the sheriff."

Sheriff Hartmann knocked at the door of the Fair Oaks Guest House. Mrs. Tuttle appeared, wiping her hands on her apron. "Yes?"

"I'm Sheriff Hartmann, Mrs. Tuttle. Is this where Joe Treddick lives?"

"Yes," said Mrs. Tuttle. "But he's not here just now. You'll have to call back."

"Do you know where he is?"

"I've no idea," said Mrs. Tuttle. "Now, if you'll excuse me."

"Thank you, Mrs. Tuttle."

Sheriff Hartmann returned to his car. On Conroy Avenue Carr Pendry's Jaguar appeared in the rearview mirror. And when Sheriff Hartmann swung into the Hovard driveway, Carr whipped the Jag smartly in after. He joined Sheriff Hartmann on the porch.

"Hello Sheriff. What's up?"

Hartmann hesitated. "Well, Carr — in confidence, there's been a break in the case. Have you seen Joe Treddick around anywhere?"

"Joe? Not today. What do you want with Joe?"

Sheriff Hartmann hesitated once more, then said, "We've got the idea that Treddick possibly knew Robert Struve in Korea."

Carr digested the information. "Golly, if Struve is dead — and Treddick shows up here — what does it mean?"

"That's what we intend to find out," said Hartmann.

Carr opened the door. "Hello," he called. "Anybody home?"

"In here," came Darrell Hovard's voice from the living room. "Who is it? Carr?"

"Carr and Sheriff Hartmann."

Darrell and Margaret were sitting quietly at the far end of the room.

"Come on in... Sit down." Darrell made a move toward the sideboard. "What'll it be — a Martini?"

"Not just now, thanks," said Hartmann. "I'm looking for Joe Treddick. Is he here?"

"Joe? What do you want Joe for?"

"Just a question or two. Is he around?"

"No," said Darrell. "He and Julie went out riding — an hour or two ago. They said they'd be back for dinner."

"Where did they go?" asked Hartmann.

"Is it — urgent?" Darrell asked in a husky voice.

"Yes, very urgent. May I use your telephone?" Hartmann asked.

Chapter XIV

Joe Treddick and Julie drove up the road past secluded ranches, a rambling old roadhouse. They angled up over the ridge and the setting sun shone point-blank into their faces. Joe slowed. They looked out over vast Silverado Valley, now swimming with golden murk.

A truck chugged up the road, passed, whined down the grade in second. The sound died away.

Joe turned into a side road leading out on the spur of a hill.

"Joe," said Julie, "Mother'll be furious if we're late for dinner."

Joe nodded, and stopped the car. They sat looking at the sunset.

A buzzard floating far out over the valley swept closer and closer, circled, slanted down and away.

Joe was holding Julie's hand. There was pulse in the grip, a warmth.

"Do you feel that?" Joe asked in strange excitement. "It's like a spark that jumps. Do you feel it?"

"Oh — more or less."

"That's life. You and I are alive."

Julie stirred, looked away, a yeasty unrest inside her. They sat in silence while the sun sank behind the hills. Julie stole a look at Joe; he was staring into the west as if he had never before seen the sun go down.

"Joe — what's worrying you?"

Joe smiled faintly, as she knew he would; he always kept his troubles to himself. "Why do you ask that?"

"You're acting so strangely. I hardly know you."

"Who knows anybody?"

"Now, Joe. For all practical purposes I know you very well."

Joe was smiling again. "You're on the verge of knowing me better."

Julie laughed uneasily. “Maybe I’d rather keep my illusions.” She looked at her watch. “Also, Mother’s going to skin us both when we wander in an hour late for dinner.”

Joe made no move to start the car.

Julie compressed her mouth in exasperation, then felt sudden compassion. Whatever was on Joe’s mind must be very important to him; usually he went out of his way to be considerate. “Bother Mother. I don’t care if we are late.”

Joe put his arm around her, drew her toward him; but she held back. She felt nervous and tense.

“Please Joe. Not now.”

They looked into each other’s faces. Joe opened his mouth, closed it; it was as if he were struggling to speak against an impediment. Julie was puzzled.

“Julie,” said Joe, “I’ve loved you from the first day I set eyes on you.”

“That’s nice.” Laughing uneasily, Julie tried to pry loose from his arm. “Let go, Joe! I don’t like to be clamped like this.”

His face was pale, set; his eyes shone.

She finally squirmed out from under his arm. From opposite sides of the car, they looked at each other.

Julie turned away. He kept sitting against the door on his side of the car, watching her. The silence between them grew tauter by the minute. What’s wrong with him? Julie thought fretfully. She reached forward, turned on the radio.

“Joe,” said Julie, “let’s go home.”

Joe was looking in the rearview mirror. “Yeah,” he said. “That’s a good idea.” He started the car, backed around. A white and black sedan was in their way — the highway patrol. An officer jumped out, waved them to a halt. He looked into the car.

“You’re Joe Treddick?”

“That’s right.”

“And you’re Miss Julie Hovard?”

“Yes.”

“What’s the trouble?” asked Joe.

“No trouble,” said the patrolman. “Would you mind waiting here just a few minutes?”

"I should be getting home," said Julie.

The patrolman returned to his car, got inside, spoke into his mike. A hollow voice rattled back. The patrolman hung up the mike.

Joe started to open the door; Julie caught his arm. "What are you going to do?"

"I want to find out what's going on."

"Wait Joe... Let's just wait..."

He relaxed into the seat.

"What on earth could they want?" Julie asked.

Joe shrugged. Julie looked at him in sudden speculation.

Five minutes passed. A second patrol car nosed down the road, stopped beside the first. Two more patrolmen got out, conferred briefly with the first; then all three came over to Joe's car.

"Mr. Treddick," said the sergeant who had arrived in the second car, "if you don't mind, I'll ride with you back to San Giorgio. Miss Hovard will go in the patrol car. Something's come up the sheriff wants to ask you about."

"What are they talking about?" Julie asked.

"Please, Miss Hovard. Out of the car."

Julie got out; the sergeant slipped into her place. "Now, Treddick, back to San Giorgio, and take it easy."

Joe started the car. "Am I under arrest?"

"You're not under arrest. Get moving."

Nineteen minutes later the patrol car delivered Julie to her front door. She jumped out and ran up the front steps. Darrell and Margaret came out; Margaret folded her in her arms.

"Julie, darling, thank God you're all right."

"Of course I'm all right," Julie snapped. "Why shouldn't I be?"

"Come in the house," said Carr, taking her arm. "I'll tell you all about it."

"Stop tugging at me," said Julie. She marched into the house. "I wish I knew what all this fuss is about..."

Sheriff Hartmann was leaning back in his swivel chair, teetering placidly, his hat on his head.

Joe came stiffly into the room. The deputy stood in the doorway. "This is Joe Treddick, Sheriff."

"Good," said Hartmann, hunching forward in his chair. "Send in some coffee, will you Howard? How about you young fellow?"

"Black," said Joe. "No sugar."

"Okay. Two java." The deputy started to close the door.

"Hey!" the sheriff called. "Send Sid in to take a statement."

"Anything else? Need the rubber hose?"

Sheriff Hartmann smiled. "Not tonight. We're going to get along, Joe and me."

The door closed. "Sorry to have made such an all-fired production of this, Joe — but we got an idea you can help us out."

"How?"

"Just answering a few questions... Have a cigarette?"

Joe accepted one with a saturnine grin.

The sheriff held out a match. "How do you like your job, Joe?"

"It's a little monotonous."

"You get a veteran's pension, don't you?"

"Not that I know of."

"I thought all prisoners-of-war got a pension."

"I suppose some do, some don't..."

A thin man with black hair parted in the middle slipped into the room, took a seat at a desk, arranged a pad.

"That's Sid," said the sheriff. "He's taking down your statement."

"Statement about what?"

"There's been a couple nasty killings around town. We're anxious to get to the bottom of them."

"I imagine you would be."

"Know anything about these killings?" asked Hartmann.

"Only what I read in the papers."

The sheriff nodded. "I see. Now, we figure that a fella named Robert Struve could give us some information." The deputy came in carrying two cups of coffee, put one in front of the sheriff, one in front of Joe.

"Thanks," said Joe.

"Thanks Howard," said Sheriff Hartmann. "Now, Joe, we hear that you served under Struve in Korea."

The sheriff waited. Joe sipped at his coffee. "Well?" the sheriff demanded.

"You're saying it," said Joe.

Hartmann frowned, then a soft smile washed across his face. "Okay, Joe. We'll play it your way. You say you knew Struve?"

Joe paused, drank his coffee, considered. The sheriff waited, watching closely. From his desk in the shadows Sid, the stenographer, watched, like a cockroach peering from a crack.

The sheriff presently said, "You're not helping yourself Joe. If you're an honest man you've got nothing to fear."

"That's why I'm not scared," said Joe.

"Good," said the sheriff heartily. "Now maybe you'll answer this question. Did you know Robert Struve in Korea?"

"Yeah," said Joe. "I knew Struve. Corporal Robert Struve."

"Ah," said Sheriff Hartmann. "Now we're getting somewhere. Just what happened to Struve?"

"The Army says he's dead. I guess that must be right."

"Hmmm," said Sheriff Hartmann. "Do you think you'd recognize a picture of Struve?"

"Hard to say."

"Look at this one." The sheriff tossed him a photograph mounted between two plates of glass. Joe ducked. The photograph fell to the floor with a clatter.

"Hell!" cried Sheriff Hartmann. "Can't you catch?"

"I'm a little nervous," said Joe.

"You're nervous all right. Like a piece of cold codfish."

Joe bent over the photograph. It was lying face down. He caught under the edge with his fingernail, flipped it over.

The face in the photograph was that of Robert Struve on his admittance to the Las Lomas Detention Home. Sheriff Hartmann, watching closely, thought he detected a quiver in Joe's cheek.

"Recognize him?"

"That's not Struve the last time I saw him."

"No? Well, well." The sheriff got to his feet. "Do you have any objection to letting us check your fingerprints?"

"Yes. I do."

The sheriff raised a finger to Sid. "Change that Sid. Make what he said, 'No, of course not'."

"Got it," said Sid.

The sheriff walked to the door. "Howard, bring in the gear."

Joe made no resistance. His fingers were inked and rolled, one after the other.

"Now, Joe, if you'll just sit tight here a minute or two... Keep an eye on him, Sid."

The sheriff left the room. Joe stubbed out his cigarette, sipped his coffee. Three minutes passed. The sheriff returned.

"Well Joe, your prints are very interesting." Joe said nothing. Hartmann lowered himself into his swivel chair. "Yep. Kinda queer coincidence, isn't it? Your prints being so much like Struve's."

Joe grinned.

"You rather be called Joe Treddick than Struve?"

"Much rather. It happens to be my name."

The sheriff leaned back in his chair. "Look, Joe — or Robert — why don't you save us both lots of trouble and tell us what happened."

"You're asking the questions."

"Why did you kill Cathy McDermott? Why did you kill Lucia Small?"

The questioning went on, until the sheriff was red-eyed and blustering; Joe Treddick, a hollow-cheeked, glassy-eyed shape.

At an early hour in the morning the sheriff made a weary gesture. "Okay Howard, take him away. Put him on ice."

"Just a moment," said Joe in a husky voice. "Am I under arrest?"

"You sure as hell are."

"What for?"

"Now you're talking foolish."

Howard took Joe's arm. "Come along fella."

Chapter XV

Julie woke up at seven o'clock with sand in her eyelids, a dull weight at her forehead, a taste of metal in her mouth.

She raised up on her elbow and looked around the room. She thought, What am I supposed to do today? What's happening... Everything came to her at once, a whole panorama of knowledge.

After a few minutes she climbed out of bed, showered, brushed her teeth, dressed in a pale blue-green cotton skirt, a white blouse, white socks, white moccasins.

She went down to breakfast. Her mother was still in bed, her father had left. The maid brought Julie orange juice, coffee, a warm raisin bun and butter.

Julie ate, then went to the phone.

"Carr, this is Julie."

"Hello Julie. What are you doing?"

"Just finishing breakfast."

"Suppose I come over."

"All right." Julie hung up. Carr, for all his conceit, was solid and predictable. Carr was—well, he was Carr. He could never have lived a secret, bitter existence. Pretending, scheming, counterfeiting. Julie's stomach gave a lurch of sheer nausea...

Carr joined her at the breakfast table. Julie brought Carr a cup and the maid poured coffee.

Carr was wearing a new suit this morning, a hard olive-tan twill, a white shirt, a black knit tie. His sandy-brown hair was smartly brushed, his round face glowed from a close shave.

"Well, Julie, this is a terrible business."

From his manner Julie knew there was something to come. "Have you heard anything new?"

Carr nodded. "I called Hartmann, and it's astounding. They took Treddick's prints. They're the same as Struve's."

Julie drank her coffee. Carr looked faintly hurt. He had expected more of a response. "Well," said Carr, "you don't seem surprised."

Julie looked away. "It's one of those things you don't really know or even suspect — but when you find out, you realize you've known all the time."

Carr twisted to inspect her. "How long has this state of inner certainty been with you?"

"I didn't even know I knew until you told me."

"It's an amazing situation," said Carr. "Absolutely amazing. Do you know what day it is?"

Julie looked at him blankly.

"Tuesday, July seventh. George Bavonette goes to the gas chamber tonight."

"Oh."

"I'm going down to the city," said Carr. "I'm going to get this execution put off. It's a travesty of justice."

Julie toyed with her cup. "Maybe Joe might confess... Or Robert, I guess I should call him."

"He hasn't, so far. I don't think he will."

"He's terribly stubborn. Remember how he was in school?"

"Yes," said Carr with a bitter laugh. "He still owes me for my motor-scooter."

Julie shook her head in wonder. "I don't know which of you has more of a one-track mind."

"I'm stubborn and tenacious," said Carr, "when I know I'm right. Mark my words Julie, I'll be governor of the state before I'm done!" He looked at his watch. "I have a big day ahead of me... Why don't you come along? We could have dinner out..."

Julie shook her head wistfully. "No thanks Carr."

"Be good for you," said Carr. "Buzz down in the ol' Jag, a little business, and then we've got the rest of the day to ourselves."

Julie looked at him sidewise. "I thought today you planned to move heaven and earth."

Carr said expansively, "With you along, I can move heaven and earth with one finger... Hello Mrs. Hovard." Margaret drifted into the room like a sleepwalker.

"Hello Carr... I'm glad you're here."

"I'm on my way to the city, Mrs. Hovard; I've been trying to persuade Julie to come. It would do her good."

Margaret looked toward Julie. "Why don't you go, dear?"

"Because I don't want to go," Julie said.

"Just as you like." Carr nodded to Margaret. "'Bye for now."

Carr left the room.

Margaret sank into a chair beside Julie. "I must be getting old; this business has left me just a wreck... To think that this boy who's eaten at our table — that you've gone out with —" Her voice failed her.

"Yes Mother," said Julie. "I've thought of all that myself. And a lot more..."

The sheriff was cool, polite, direct.

"Well, Struve —"

"My name is Treddick," said Joe.

"Struve — Treddick — call yourself anything you like."

"What am I being held for?"

"Don't worry about that," said Hartmann. "There's a dozen technical charges I could book you on. How about desertion from the Army?"

"You couldn't make it stick," said Joe. "My time terminated five days after I was captured."

"As Corporal Robert Struve, or as Private Joe Treddick?"

"Either one. We signed up on the same day."

"That's the right attitude, Struve."

"Treddick."

The sheriff raised his eyebrows. "How can you be Treddick when your fingerprints say you're Struve?"

"Get your stenographer in here, because I'll just tell you once."

"Okay," said Sheriff Hartmann amiably.

Sid slipped in through the door, slid into his chair.

"At one time I was Corporal Robert Struve, of the 121st Army Engineers. Five days before the end of my enlistment a mortar shell got us.

Hit us right on the nose. I was down in the creek bed and the explosion went over my head. Otherwise, it busted the platoon. Arms, legs everywhere. I was due to get out; remember this. I did nothing wrong. But I was sick of Robert Struve. I wanted to be somebody else. Robert Struve is the face in that picture you showed me."

"Yeah," said Hartmann. "Go on. This is interesting."

"Maybe I'd been waiting for a chance; maybe I was battle-happy. I don't know. What happened was I picked up Treddick's dog tag, gave mine to what was left of Joe. I didn't really figure out what I was going to do. The way it turned out, I didn't have to. The Commies came over the hill; they took me away. From then on, I was Joe Treddick."

"Kinda tough on Treddick's folks, wasn't it?"

"He didn't have folks. Third cousins in Boston; that's all. Also, Joe was getting his discharge the same time I was getting mine.

"To make a long story short, I got away from the Commies. I hid out two days and three nights and finally made it back to our own lines. I had a broken arm and an infection where the shrapnel nicked me in the neck. I went to the hospital and never did get back to my own outfit."

"That was kinda lucky for you," said Hartmann.

"It wouldn't have made any real difference. I wasn't trying to pull anything. It was just a gesture —"

"So that's why you came back to San Giorgio?"

"Sheriff, you wouldn't understand why I came back to San Giorgio if I told you."

"Try me."

"I lived in San Giorgio fourteen years. I got to know certain people. They knew me as Robert Struve. I wanted to come back and know them as Joe Treddick, somebody other than the town monster."

The sheriff thought about it, and nodded. "Go on with your story. You were in the hospital."

"I took my discharge in Japan, signed on a Panamanian freighter, and came back to the States the long way. In New York I legally changed my name to Joe Treddick. That's my name today."

"What about the Army?"

"That score is even. Struve for Treddick."

"What if they found out?"

"If they find out, I tell them about the mix-up in dog tags."

"You're willing to let another man go to the gas chamber for a crime you committed?"

Joe looked surprised. "What crime is this?"

"You killed Dean Bavonette. George Bavonette takes the rap."

Joe laughed shortly. "Seems to me he confessed."

"Okay. Why did you cut up Cathy McDermott and Lucia Small?"

"Are you accusing me?"

"I'm just asking. Why did you do it?"

Joe lit a cigarette. "I didn't."

"Can you prove that you didn't?"

"I don't need to."

The sheriff became angry. "What do you say about this?" He opened a manila folder. Scotch-taped to the inside was a card. Letters printed in purple ink read:

HELLO ROBERT.
YOU WON'T PULL IT OFF.

"What've you got to say?"

"Nothing very much. Lucia Small sent it."

The sheriff nodded. "What's it mean?"

"She thought I was planning to marry into the Hovard family."

"Were you?"

Joe looked at him stonily. "What do you think?"

The sheriff opened another manila envelope, displayed it to Joe.

ROBERT STRUVE IS A SAVAGE LOVER.
HE CUTS THROATS AND FACES.
HE'S THE MAN TO FIND.

Joe frowned. "Where did you get this?"

"Lucia mailed it the day she was killed. To me."

"Let's see the envelope."

The sheriff tossed Joe the envelope.

Joe looked at it. "The postmark is for the day after she died."

"She probably mailed it in a box, after last pickup."

"I don't believe it. She knew I was Robert Struve."

"That's what's puzzling me," said Sheriff Hartmann. "How did she know?"

"I took her home from that Mountainview Masque. The Turrets is pretty hard to find unless you know just where to go. I drove straight out there. She said, 'How come you know this road? You're a stranger around here!'

"I couldn't give her any answer. Then she said, 'You always have looked familiar to me, in an odd kind of way.' And about two minutes later she said, 'I know who you are! You're Robert Struve!'

"I told her she was crazy, but she just laughed. It was while I was taking her home that Cathy McDermott got it. Lucia knew I was clean out of it. If she wrote that letter, it was out of spite."

"Spite? Why?"

"She wanted to park. I didn't."

The sheriff grunted. "We got the goods on you, Treddick."

Joe laughed.

"You had motive — opportunity —"

"No more motive than anybody else. And as for opportunity, I was taking Lucia home when Cathy was killed."

"That would make a good alibi — if Lucia were alive to bear you out."

"So it would."

The sheriff looked at Joe for a long minute. "Joe — you're a pretty smart boy. But I'm gonna get you for these killings."

"Okay," said Joe. "I can stand it if you can."

Julie wandered around the house. She changed into a bathing suit, walked out across the lawn to the swimming pool, where she settled into a deck chair.

Joe Treddick — Robert Struve. The two images melted, merged into each other, separated. Robert's terrible scar just wouldn't seem to fit on Joe's strong jaw and flat cheeks. Once or twice she had noticed a long mark under his chin; it must have been the edge of the skin graft.

His nose — how could Joe's short straight nose cover the black gape of Robert's nostrils? Somehow it did… Anyone could be horrible with their face cut and torn… Think of Cathy and Dean and Lucia…

Joe. Robert.

All the rest of her life those names would give her an inward stir… What would have happened if Robert had never been hurt? If she hadn't been driving the car one evening when she was eight? Five lives. Dean Pendry. Cathy McDermott. Lucia Small. George Bavonette. Robert Struve.

Joe Treddick?

Julie's thoughts faltered to a stop. Could there be good in Joe Treddick? She sighed. What a terrible force must drive him! Sharp as lightning, grinding and harsh as a bulldozer in gravel! Certainly he must feel nothing but agony at his own acts…

Margaret called her to lunch. At two, Julie walked listlessly downtown. She bought an early edition of the *Herald-Republican* and looked through the headlines for the words 'Sex Slayer'. Nothing leapt at her eyes. She looked more carefully and found a cautious half-column which quoted Sheriff Hartmann as expecting an arrest within the next twenty-four hours.

She wandered home, lay down on her bed and presently fell asleep. She woke up about four-thirty.

When she went downstairs she found her mother drinking tea with Carr Pendry.

"You got back early," said Julie, the faintest of sardonic overtones in her voice.

Carr looked tired; Julie felt immediately sorry. "Did you accomplish anything at all?"

Carr shook his head. "A stone wall — everywhere. Nobody seems to care a tinker's damn. They just look blank." He banged his fist on the table. "And you'd never guess what."

"What?"

"He's let Struve go."

"Let him go! Why?"

Carr shrugged. "Lack of evidence. It doesn't mean anything. They're just giving him rope. They'll get him."

"What a horrible creature," murmured Margaret. "I can't get over it. Here — at this very table. Eating our food."

Carr returned to the events of the day. "I spoke to the judge. He refused to see the connection between Dean's death and what's happened up here."

"Did you tell him about Robert?" Julie asked.

"Of course I told him." Carr continued, "On my way home I dropped into San Quentin and was allowed to talk to Bavonette."

"On the day he's being executed?" asked Margaret. "That sounds so morbid somehow."

Carr looked at his watch. "It's now four-thirty. In two and one half hours ... Well, as a relative — I'm his brother-in-law, after all —"

"I should think that would be more reason they wouldn't let you in," said Julie. "Brother of the girl he's supposed to have killed."

Carr frowned. "He looks terrible. Like a death's-head. His face is all caved in."

"Poor fellow," said Margaret.

"His hands are like claws," said Carr. "You've heard the expression about somebody's eyes glowing. Well, that's how Bavonette's eyes were — as if there was a little lamp in each of them."

"Did he seem pleased to see you?" Margaret asked.

"He didn't seem to care. I told him the situation, told him that even now if he'd deny that confession there might be a chance."

"What did he say?"

Carr drank his tea before replying. "He gave me the most peculiar look I've ever seen on a man's face. It was a man laughing at death, anxious for it. He's actually glad he's being killed!"

"Isn't that strange!" said Margaret.

"There's something weird involved there. He's crazy as a bedbug, of course. But he's expiating something ..."

"Just what did he say?" asked Julie.

"He told me to mind my own business. He said — let's see. His exact words were something like this. He almost sang them. Like bop music. 'Brother, this life has been one long round of hell. I've fought it on the weed. I've fought it on the piano. They say there's another life where they play harps; brother, I'm ready. You can take this one' —"

Carr broke off with a sad smile for Margaret. "He told me what I could do with it."

"The poor man is obviously crazy," Margaret said indignantly. "He should be in an institution."

Carr nodded. "Instead, they're killing him —" he looked at his watch "— in two hours and twenty-five minutes."

Julie rose to her feet. Margaret looked at her curiously. "Where are you going, dear?"

"Upstairs."

Carr jumped up. "I was going to suggest — if you'd like to go for a ride tonight, Julie —"

"No thanks," said Julie.

"Why Julie, I think it would do you good," said Margaret.

"Okay," said Julie. She turned, facing Carr. "On one condition."

"Sure. Anything you like."

"We go just where I want to go. Do what I want to do. Without argument. Is it a deal?"

"If you insist."

"Okay." Julie started from the room.

Chapter XVI

Carr took Julie's arm as they descended the steps, led her toward the Jaguar. Julie pulled back. "Let's take my car."

Carr acquiesced. "This is your evening."

Julie went to the driver's side. Carr climbed in on the right, sitting very straight, looking stiffly ahead. Julie said, "You might as well know where I'm going now, so there won't be any argument. I'm going to talk to Joe Treddick."

Carr turned his head in shock. "Julie — I don't think that's very smart."

"Okay. Do you want to come? Or do I go alone?"

"But why, Julie? Why in the name of merciful heaven?"

"I want to see him," said Julie. She shook her head. "Maybe he's a murderer — but he's honest. Anyway Carr, I want to talk to him! I've got to get straightened out!" she cried passionately. "I don't know whether I'm coming or going. If he's not a murderer, I want to know that I was right about him."

"Say he's innocent. He's still an impostor —"

She looked at him levelly. "What would you have done, Carr, if you'd had a face like Robert Struve's?"

"That's neither here nor there. I thought tonight we were going out, maybe have a drink —"

"Okay Carr. Please get out."

Carr said tersely, "I'll come."

"No more argument?"

"Anything you like."

Julie started the car, drove down Conroy Avenue, out Third Street to the Fair Oaks Guest House.

She parked, jumped out. Carr started to follow. "No," said Julie. "I want to talk to Joe, alone. I'll call you if I need you."

"Your folks would skin me alive," Carr protested in real distress. "After all, they trust me to look after you!"

"Once and for all Carr, you're along tonight for the ride. If you don't like it, you can go home."

She climbed the steps, rang the bell; Mrs. Tuttle came to the door.

"May I speak to Joe Treddick, please?"

Mrs. Tuttle looked at her in careful speculation. "You know who Joe Treddick is?"

"Certainly I know who he is."

"His real name is Robert Struve, and unless I miss my guess —"

"May I speak to him?"

Mrs. Tuttle snorted. "Do you think he'd be in my house a single minute after I found out who he was? Run along, young lady. He's not here."

"Where did he go?"

"I've not the slightest idea."

"Thank you." Julie went back to the car.

"Well?" said Carr.

"He's not there." Julie pressed the starter button.

Sheriff Hartmann was not in his office; the deputy suggested they try his home.

The sheriff lived in a new three-bedroom house in one of the developments springing up around San Giorgio. Carr agreed to ask the whereabouts of Joe Treddick. Julie went with him to the door.

In answer to the bell, Sheriff Hartmann appeared in his shirt-sleeves. When Carr made his inquiry the sheriff put on a thoughtful frown.

"Seems to me he said something about one of the motels. Just what do you want with him?"

Carr looked at Julie. "We just want to chat a bit — old times, you know."

"Oh," said the sheriff, nodding wisely.

"For the life of me," said Carr, "I can't see why you let him go!"

"For a very good reason. There's no evidence against him."

"What about all this false-name stuff, the letters —"

"That's background, Carr. A lot different from evidence. It's good for filling in the chinks and crannies of a case, but first you've got to get a case. We just don't have one. Not even the beginnings of one."

"Come on, Carr," said Julie.

He followed her sulkily back to the car. "Now where?"

"I thought we'd just run down the road, look for his car."

"Now Julie, there's a dozen motels in town — we can't explore all of them."

"I guess you're right," said Julie.

"Now where are you going?" asked Carr.

"Home."

"Home? The night's young!"

Julie said nothing. She turned up Conroy Avenue, into Jamaica Terrace and up into her driveway.

"Julie," said Carr, "this hasn't been my kind of party at all."

"What did you want to do? Neck?"

Carr stiffly opened the door. "Good night Julie... I don't think I'll come in."

"Good night Carr. I didn't ask you to."

Carr jumped into the Jaguar, started the motor, swung around, roared out the driveway and back toward town.

"Big overgrown baby," Julie muttered to herself. She started her car, quietly backed around, drove out, down to the highway.

Julie turned south. The highway led past dingy service stations, used-car lots, taverns, two veterinary hospitals.

Nothing in the Bon Haven, the San Giorgio Courts, the Kozy Kourts, or Bender's Motel. The Green Gables was past the farthest street light, out where the country began. A dozen duplex cabins with green asphalt-tile roofing surrounded a central area which once had been graveled. Two oak trees with whitewashed trunks grew in the center. The cabin marked OFFICE displayed a light; all the others seemed dark and untenanted. Julie parked off the road, walked quietly into the court.

Down at the far end she saw Joe's car. She stood looking at the cabin, wishing she had someone with her.

She went back out to the car, got in. She put the key in the lock, then hesitated. She'd come this far... Slowly she got out of the car, went back into the court, looked at the cabin.

Inside was Joe. Robert Struve. Joe. She stood looking at the blank door for two minutes. All the cabins seemed vacant except Joe's.

She went slowly up to the door, her heart pounding. She paused, her hand raised to knock. A foolish thing to do, really. But it had to be done. It was the breaking crest to a wave of events that had started ten years ago, when a little girl steered a car into a motor-scooter.

Her fist came down. She knocked.

Inside a bed creaked, feet hit the floor. The door opened.

"Hello," said Julie. "Can I come in?"

The door closed behind her with a soft sound. Four candles burned on the bedside table. There was no light in the room other than the glow from the four flames.

Julie looked around in quizzical curiosity. "Why the candles?"

"Just a whim." Joe sat down on the bed. "Have a seat."

Julie moved a cane-bottomed rocker around, settled herself. They looked at each other. The candles cast a rich paleness on one side of their faces, left the other side in velvet-black shadow.

"Well Robert?" said Julie in a soft voice.

"My name is Joe Treddick."

Joe stared at her. Julie saw that he had lost weight. His face looked thin.

"You're a strange creature, Robert."

Once more, he said, "My name is Joe Treddick."

Julie made a sound of scornful amusement. "Just how dumb do you think I am?"

"Oh — medium."

"How about yourself? What do you think of yourself?"

"I try to avoid it." He swung his legs up, lay back on the bed, lit a cigarette. "I suppose you're entitled to an explanation."

Julie waited. Her courage was beginning to thin out. She became conscious of her youth, her inexperience, her lack of toughness. Then she hardened. She had nothing to be ashamed of. Let him lie there, with as much flinty self-assurance as he cared to assume... Joe was speaking.

"As far as I'm concerned, Robert Struve died in Korea. I never cared much for Robert. Mother-ridden little mollycoddle."

The dispassionate contempt startled Julie. She felt an impulse to defend Robert Struve. She remembered the Robert Struve she had known in high school — the boy who had played football like a maniac, who studied like a monk, who made no friends and walked by himself. Mother-ridden mollycoddle? Hardly!

"Joe Treddick was a different kind of man," said Joe. "He did things because he liked them. I changed my name. I'm Joe Treddick. Now I do things because I like to do them."

"Such as — murder?"

Joe puffed thoughtfully on his cigarette; the smoke spiraled toward the ceiling. The candles flickered.

Joe said, "You've got me arrested, tried, sentenced, hanged, and buried out of sight — even before you ask whether or not I'm guilty."

"Is there any question? All this sneaking around, this — maneuvering, coming up here under false pretenses."

"My name is Joe Treddick. If you'd asked me about Struve, I would have told you. But Struve is dead. Joe Treddick is alive. I took no unfair advantage of you or anyone else."

Julie leaned forward, her voice passionate. "How about Dean Pendry? George Bavonette died two hours ago. You murdered him just like you murdered his wife." Joe started to speak but Julie rushed on. "I know why you did it. Four girls at the Tri-Gamma initiation. Dean, Cathy, Lucia, me. Four silly little girls. They hurt your feelings. And you got your revenge."

Joe was grinning painfully. "Do you honestly believe that?"

"I know what you did to me."

"Yeah," said Joe. "I paid for it... I'm sorry about that."

"Your apology comes five years late."

"Better late than never."

"How about Dean? I suppose you didn't wreck her home."

Joe laughed shortly.

"Well?"

Joe shrugged. "I saw Dean in a bar on Market Street in San Francisco. I knew her; she didn't know me. I made a pickup. Maybe the idea of revenge entered into it. I suppose it did. She never mentioned she was married — with her husband banging the piano not twenty feet away. When I found she was married, I laid off. I saw her twice after that. The last time was the night she was killed. That's when she recognized me."

Julie looked at him. "It's a wonder I never did."

"She saw me with the bottom of my face behind a magazine. I was reading. She stopped in the middle of the room, and told me I was stubborn and had no soul — that I reminded her of a boy she used to know in high school — a horrible boy named Robert Struve. She looked again." Joe laughed shortly. "Her eyes were the size of pie plates. She ran into her bedroom. I left."

Julie held up her hand, blocking the bottom of Joe's face from her vision. He was suddenly Robert Struve. She took away her hand. He was Joe again.

"The next-to-last time I saw Dean was up on Telegraph Hill. You and Cathy were there. In Cholo's apartment."

Julie was startled. "I didn't notice you."

"I noticed you. I knew who you were right away." He sat up on the bed. "And I knew right away what I wanted out of life — more than anything else. You. I made sure of a seat next to you in English 1B. I wanted a fair chance at you, on even terms with everyone else — without the past hung around my neck like an albatross."

Julie said in a subdued voice, "That's all very well — but Dean? Why did she have to die?"

"Do you mean, why did I kill her?"

"Yes."

He laughed bitterly. "Could it be possible that the man who got executed for Dean's murder was the man that did it?"

"I've thought about it... But there's Cathy and Lucia."

"Why pick on me?"

"You had the motive."

Joe laughed. "And five years later I cut their throats?"

Julie was silent.

"Sure," said Joe. "At the time my feelings were hurt. I was going to make lots of money, get a handsome face. They'd fall in love with me, come on their hands and knees crying for a kind look. Then I'd jilt 'em."

Joe put on a tired smile. "Those were daydreams. I got over them about the same time I joined the Army."

"You tell a good story, Joe."

He turned his head quickly. "You called me Joe."

"Yes, what of it?"

"That means you believe me."

Julie looked away, watched the candles. "I never did — completely — have you hanged, drawn and quartered."

He looked at her curiously. "Did you come alone?"

"Yes."

"Does anyone know you're here?"

"No."

"You're a trusting little soul." He put out his cigarette. "Suppose I'm the San Giorgio murderer after all?"

She moved in the chair, looked down at her hands. She was blushing.

He rose to his feet, went to look at the candles. She came slowly across the room, stood beside him. Her flesh was tingling, her mouth dry. "Inside," she said, "I suppose we're all a little strange…"

He looked down at her, his eyebrows arched, his mouth tight. He put his arm around her. The touch was like a spring; the tenseness went out of Julie; she leaned against Joe, and the strange inner feelings gave way to warmth and quiet. She put her arm around him and together they stood looking into the flames.

"Will you marry me Julie?"

"As soon as I'm eighteen."

Presently Julie asked, "Why the candles Joe?"

"It's a demonstration."

He reached to the dresser, picked up a glossy 8" × 10" photograph. "Look at this."

Julie took the photograph. "Well?"

It was one of the pictures which had appeared on the *Herald-Republican* society page: the bar at Mountainview Masque, with Joe and Lucia near the door.

"What do you see?"

She studied it in the light of the four candles. "Only what we saw the other day. With more detail of course…Oh. The candles!"

"Right," said Joe. "I can measure how long they are in this photograph."

"How? How can you be sure —"

"The label on this bottle of Scotch is exactly four inches high. I measured it this evening in a liquor store. That gives me a scale to measure the candles with. These new ones here —" he pointed "— are twelve inches long. These in the holder are all a little less than six and a half inches long. Say six and three-eighths. In other words, they've burned five and five-eighths inches."

"I see," said Julie. "And now — you're checking how long it takes for these to burn five and five-eighths inches."

"That's right." He laid a steel tape along the side of the candle, measured, looked at his watch. "It works out just about an inch and a half to the hour. Five and five-eighths divided by one and a half." He calculated further. "Three and three-quarters hours."

"Mrs. Hutson lit those candles," said Julie. "We got there about eight-thirty. And she'd just finished."

"Eight-thirty. Add three and three-quarters hours. Twelve-fifteen. That cinches it," said Joe. "This photograph was taken at quarter after twelve. I couldn't possibly have taken Lucia home and gotten back before one. It lets me out."

"Shall we call the sheriff?"

Joe looked toward the dresser, for a reason Julie could not fathom at the time. "He'll find out soon enough."

Julie laughed. "What's the joke?" asked Joe.

"Mother thinks you're the devil incarnate."

Joe grinned. "She'll never forgive me."

She put her arms around him. "Joe, do you think you can go on loving me? I'm such a spoiled brat."

"I think it'll work out."

"Remember the night I telephoned you — the first night we went out?"

"Yes."

"I told Cathy that I was going to marry you." Julie's face fell. "Poor Cathy... Joe — who did kill her?"

Joe looked at her in surprise. "Do you mean you don't know?"

"Of course not!"

"But it's obvious."

"Well — tell me. Don't be mysterious."

"Dean Bavonette told Carr she had seen Robert Struve. Dean was killed; Carr was sure that Struve had hacked up his sister. He was very much upset when the police arrested George. That meant that Struve was getting away with something. The idea just about drove him nuts. He's always hated me.

"On the night of the Masque he got a little tight. He parked with Cathy, probably began pawing her."

Julie nodded. "And Cathy told him to stop — that was the mood she was in."

"Then Carr got mad. Maybe she threatened to tell, maybe he killed her out of jealousy. But she was dead. Carr had a problem: how to get out from under? And he thought of Dean. If Robert Struve had hacked up Dean — why couldn't Robert Struve be blamed for hacking up Cathy? So he takes his pocket knife and goes to work. When he's all done, he bangs his head somewhere — maybe on the bumper — smears himself with dust and gore, comes staggering back claiming someone hit him on the head. Next day he says this man is Robert Struve. The joke is that I'm standing there all the time. I know Carr is lying. It's an absolute cinch that he's done it himself."

"Lucia knew who you were — so she knew Carr was lying, too."

Joe nodded. "She figured she'd have some fun writing letters. She figured wrong. Carr fixed her, too. Then to set the sheriff after Struve, he prints a letter with Lucia's equipment, and mails it."

The door opened. Carr edged into the room. "I heard what you said about me." He looked at Julie. His round face was flushed and twisted. It looked purple in the candlelight. "I thought I'd find you! You wouldn't go out with *me* —"

Julie pressed back against Joe, watching Carr as if he were something weird disguised as a man.

"You believe this liar, this impostor!" cried Carr. "You take his word ahead of mine!"

"It's not a matter of taking his word," said Julie. "He couldn't have done it. He wasn't there when it happened."

"He was there! He hit me on the head — all his life he's tried to get the best of me!" Carr looked from one to the other. "Julie — I'm about to pay you the most extreme compliment I can think of." Carr blew out his cheeks. "I want you to be Mrs. Carr Pendry. I want you to be my wife."

Julie laughed — a breathless half-hysterical titter.

"Well, Julie?" Carr was his most pompous self.

"You've got to wait your turn. Joe asked me first."

"Don't be funny," growled Carr. He took a gun from his coat pocket.

"Carr!" said Julie. "That's my gun! You took it out of my car! Give it to me this instant!"

And it seemed as if Carr were ready to obey. He leaned forward — but reconsidered. "No Julie. Struve here thinks he can wriggle free."

"But he didn't do anything!"

"All his life he's worked against me. I'm going to show him it doesn't pay."

"How?" Joe asked.

Carr grinned, moved the automatic. "Tomorrow they'll find you two in here. You'll be shot — with this gun. Julie'll be holding the gun; you'll have a knife. They'll think that you started to cut her — and then she shot you."

"That's a nice idea," said Joe.

"Oh, I'm getting to be a connoisseur in these things," said Carr. "This'll be the third."

"The future governor of the state talking," said Joe.

Carr looked disturbed. "So what? Who's going to know?"

"First," said Joe, "there's yourself."

"I'm not going to tell," grinned Carr.

"Then there's the deputy sheriff in the cabin next-door. He's catching it all on a tape recorder."

Carr was suddenly pale. "Deputy sheriff?"

"Certainly. His name is Clifford. You don't think Hartmann would let me run around loose, do you?"

Carr looked around the room. "This cabin isn't wired."

"The bug's behind the dresser, in case you're interested. The wire runs through the corner behind the molding."

Carr sidled across the room, the gun pointed at Joe. He pushed the dresser away from the wall, glanced behind it. "There's nothing here."

"Look on this side," said Joe.

Carr stepped around the front of the dresser. He shoved the dresser out from the other wall, glanced into the gap. Candlelight glinted on metal. Carr stared down at the microphone; it winked back up at him. He stood like a man entranced. Julie reached out, gave Carr a push. He lurched into the gap behind the dresser, tried to brace himself with the hand holding the gun. Joe crushed the wrist across the corner of the dresser, wrenched away the gun.

Carr slowly pulled himself out of the gap.

"Just sit in that rocking chair," said Joe, "or I'll have to shoot you in the knee. And that hurts."

The door opened. Clifford, the deputy sheriff, came in behind a big .45. "Everybody sit or stand just exactly like they are."

"It's safe now," said Joe.

"I wasn't worried about safety," said Clifford. "I just wanted to get as much of that on tape as I could."

"And in the meantime," said Julie, "Carr cuts a couple more throats."

"You trying to tell me my business, young lady? Now you run across to the saloon and call the sheriff."

The rising sun shone in their faces.

"Five-thirty," said Julie. "We made good time." She patted the dashboard. "Good old Plymouth… And what are you grinning about?" she asked Joe.

"I'm just wondering how long before your father and mother will speak to me."

"They'll speak when I tell them to," said Julie. "I'm one day older than eighteen, and if nothing else in the world I'm going to pick my own husband."

A large sign arched over the road ahead of them. It read:

RENO CITY LIMITS

THE BIGGEST LITTLE CITY
IN THE WORLD

"Oh, Joe," said Julie, "I'm so happy."

Joe took her hand and kissed it. "I am too."

"What'll we do first? Eat breakfast or get married?"

"Are you hungry?"

"Ravenous."

"Let's eat first, and then we won't have to get the judge out of bed."

They passed another sign:

❀ ORANGE BLOSSOM CHAPEL ❀

Marriages Performed Any Hour of
Day or Night

ONE HUNDRED YARDS ON THE RIGHT

"Oh, hell," said Joe. "Let's get married first. We can always eat."

Afterword and Afterward

The Flesh Mask, as a tale of a disguised man seeking revenge for his earlier torture by respectable people, owes a great deal to *The Count of Monte Cristo* (1844). In that massive adventure novel, a young man is arrested on fabricated charges and imprisoned in the Chateau d'If, located on an isle in the Mediterranean. A fellow prisoner helps the hero by not only deducing the identities of the treacherous trio who had set him up for such a terrible fate, but also by giving him the map to a secret treasure, and finally by giving him an escape route from the jail. The hero, having gained his freedom, fashions a new persona as the Count of Monte Cristo, and then sets out to avenge himself.

Jack Vance used "The Count" on more than one occasion across his career. The most famous example is the Demon Princes series, where the avenger Kirth Gersen stalks interstellar crime lords across five novels. Kirth Gersen uses detective skills, financial manipulations, and corporate takeovers, all methods used by The Count.

The Count has a less pronounced presence in the Alastor Cluster and the Durdane series, but invisible avengers still lurk in the background: both works have government leaders (the Connatic and the Faceless Man, respectively) traveling in disguise and dispensing justice among their citizens. (In fact, "Alastor" is Greek for "avenger.")

Vance aficionados will have already picked up the name "Chateau d'If" mentioned a few paragraphs before, since this is the title of an early Vance novella published in 1950 as an open allusion to The Count. While Chateau d'If is a real fortress on a real island, Vance playfully reuses the name as if it meant what it sounds like in English: the House of "What If?" For the first few chapters of Vance's story it seems that this place name is the only link to The Count, but then it changes into a full-bore homage.

In addition to all this matter relating to The Count, *The Flesh Mask* is an early study on Vance and masks. Sometimes the masks in a Vancean fiction are literal, as in the celebrated novelette "The Moon Moth" (1961), where respectable people wear multiple masks based upon their social status. In "Chateau d'If" the mask is a full body transfer. But at other times the masks are more figurative, as in the multiple roles played by the villain in *The Palace of Love* (1967) and by every citizen of Kirstendale on *Big Planet* (1957).

Vance's career as a mystery writer saw a burst of activity in the late 1950s as he produced a total of seven novels. He reworked earlier pieces so that *Cold Fish* led to *The Flesh Mask,* and *Courage My Strange Child,* another lost novel, contributed to *Strange People, Queer Notions* (1985). Then there was *Bird Island* (1957), written in 1947. Beyond these three cases from the 1940s came four new works: *Bad Ronald* (1973) written in 1955; *The House on Lily Street* (1979) written in 1958; *The View from Chickweed's Window* (1979) probably written in 1959; and Vance's big hit *The Man in the Cage* (1960), likely written in 1958. These seven books amount to half of his mystery novel output, including the three Ellery Queen titles.

It seems that from the beginning Jack Vance pursued a career in mystery, parallel to his work in science fiction and fantasy. It makes good sense for an author to keep his options open to different genres in this way, and *The Flesh Mask* represents the early fruit from Vance's work in mystery.

—Michael Andre-Driussi

About the Author

Jack Vance was born in 1916 to a well-off California family that, as his childhood ended, fell upon hard times. As a young man he worked at a series of unsatisfying jobs before studying mining engineering, physics, journalism and English at the University of California Berkeley. Leaving school as America was going to war, he found a place as an ordinary seaman in the merchant marine. Later he worked as a rigger, surveyor, ceramicist, and carpenter before his steady production of sf, mystery novels, and short stories established him as a full-time writer.

His output over more than sixty years was prodigious and won him three Hugo Awards, a Nebula Award, a World Fantasy Award for lifetime achievement, as well as an Edgar from the Mystery Writers of America. The Science Fiction and Fantasy Writers of America named him a grandmaster and he was inducted into the Science Fiction Hall of Fame.

His works crossed genre boundaries, from dark fantasies (including the highly influential *Dying Earth* cycle of novels) to interstellar space operas, from heroic fantasy (the *Lyonesse* trilogy) to murder mysteries featuring a sheriff (the Joe Bain novels) in a rural California county. A Vance story often centered on a competent male protagonist thrust into a dangerous, evolving situation on a planet where adventure was his daily fare, or featured a young person setting out on a perilous odyssey over difficult terrain populated by entrenched, scheming enemies.

Late in his life, a world-spanning assemblage of Vance aficionados came together to return his works to their original form, restoring material cut by editors whose chief preoccupation was the page count of a pulp magazine. The result was the complete and authoritative *Vance Integral Edition* in 44 hardcover volumes. Spatterlight Press is now publishing the VIE texts as ebooks, and as print-on-demand paperbacks.

Colophon

This book was printed using Adobe Arno Pro as the primary text font, with NeutraFace used on the cover.

This title was created from the digital archive of the Vance Integral Edition, a series of 44 books produced under the aegis of the author by a worldwide group of his readers. The VIE project gratefully acknowledges the editorial guidance of Norma Vance, as well as the cooperation of the Department of Special Collections at Boston University, whose John Holbrook Vance collection has been an important source of textual evidence.

Special thanks to R.C. Lacovara, Patrick Dusoulier, Koen Vyverman, Paul Rhoads, Chuck King, Gregory Hansen, Suan Yong, and Josh Geller for their invaluable assistance preparing final versions of the source files.

Digitize: Richard Chandler, Joel Hedlund, Andreas Irle, Paul Rhoads; Diff: Damien G. Jones, Paul Rhoads; Tech Proof: Rob Friefeld; Text Integrity: Paul Rhoads, Norma Vance; Compose: Andreas Irle; Comp Review: John A.D. Foley, Marcel van Genderen, Charles King, Paul Rhoads, Robin L. Rouch; Update Verify: John A. D. Foley, Marcel van Genderen, Charles King; RTF-Diff: Charles King, Bill Schaub; Textport: Patrick Dusoulier; Proofread: Erik Arendse, Angus Campbell-Cann, Jurgen Devriese, Marcel van Genderen, Jasper Groen, Patrick Hudson, Jurriaan Kalkman, Paul Rhoads, Willem Timmer, Hans van der Veeke, Dirk Jan Verlinde, Koen Vyverman

Artwork (maps based on original drawings by Jack and Norma Vance):

Paul Rhoads, Christopher Wood

Book Composition and Typesetting: Joel Anderson

Art Direction and Cover Design: Howard Kistler

Proofing: Steve Sherman, Dave Worden

Jacket Blurb: Steve Sherman, John Vance

Management: John Vance, Koen Vyverman

Printed in Great Britain
by Amazon